THE

Wizard's

REVENGE

Dear Mark & Ali,

The wizard has some pretty nasty tricks up his sleeve in this story.

Love and Blessings,

Patty old West

VOLUME ELEVEN

THE

Wizard's

REVENGE

The Twith Logue Chronicles
Adventures with the Little People

KENNETH G. OLD
& PATTY OLD WEST

TATE PUBLISHING
AND ENTERPRISES, LLC

Published by Tate Publishing & Enterprises, LLC
127 E. Trade Center Terrace | Mustang, Oklahoma 73064 USA
1.888.361.9473 | www.tatepublishing.com

Tate Publishing is committed to excellence in the publishing industry. The company reflects the philosophy established by the founders, based on Psalm 68:11,
"The Lord gave the word and great was the company of those who published it."

Book design copyright © 2014 by Tate Publishing, LLC. All rights reserved.
Cover design by Jeffrey Doblados
Interior design by Gram Telen
Poetry excerpts from Footprints in the Dust by Kenneth G. Old
Map design by Rich and Lisa Ballou

Published in the United States of America

ISBN: 978-1-62854-229-5
1. Fiction / Fantasy / General
2. Fiction / General
14.01.22

DEDICATION

Ken spinning tales of the Little People to children gathered on Sandes Hill

Dedicated to the children who first heard these stories
at the boarding school in Murree, Pakistan.

OTHER BOOKS BY KENNETH G. OLD

Walking the Way
Footprints in the Dust
A Boy and His Lunch
So Great a Cloud
Roses for a Stranger
The Wizard of Wozzle
Squidgy on the Brook
Gibbins Brook Farm
The Wizard Strikes Twice
Beyonders in Gyminge
The SnuggleWump Roars
The Secret Quest
Dayko's Rime
Circus in Sellindge
The Magician's Twitch

OTHER BOOKS BY PATTY OLD WEST

Good and Faithful Servant
Once Met, Never Forgotten
The Wizard of Wozzle
Squidgy on the Brook
Gibbins Brook Farm
The Wizard Strikes Twice
Beyonders in Gyminge
The SnuggleWump Roars
The Secret Quest
Dayko's Rime
Circus in Sellindge
The Magician's Twitch

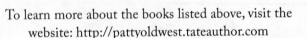

To learn more about the books listed above, visit the
website: http://pattyoldwest.tateauthor.com

EAGLE'S FLIGHT

Better grasp at a flying star
Than seize the sweet fruit on the bough.
Better than walking tall, by far,
Is to soar with the eagles now.

When there is a chance to choose
There are things only birds can see.
Better by far wings than shoes.
Alas, earthbound mortals are we.

Better a child's mind set alight
With fantasy's call to be free
Than a hundred facts put right
To maintain its captivity.

Acknowledgments

Ken Old was a man of many talents. The Lord endowed him with the ability to see beyond the everyday and gave him the creative writing talent to put those dreams and visions onto paper. His unique way of looking at things opens up new vistas of imagination beyond the ordinary. It is my hope that while reading about the Little People, you can capture some of that same exciting, vibrant, carefree way of living and seeing.

Special thanks go to Margaret Spoelman, Patrick Wilburn, and Kim Dang for kindly making copies of the first chapters Gumpa sent by e-mail. After being entered into the computer, Gumpa's creative genius generated more than would fit into one book. It was split, and the two smaller stories were expanded once again. Those also became too large and had to be divided. Eventually, the initial few chapters became twelve volumes known as The *Twith Logue Chronicles*. They chronicle the adventures of the Little People as they are exiled from their homeland until they are able to return many centuries later.

It is with heartfelt gratitude and much appreciation that I acknowledge my darling daughters: Sandy Gaudette, Becky Shupe and Karin Spanner, who were involved in all stages of the editing process. From ensuring that Jock's Scottish dialogue was correct to the final proof reading, each gave me valuable assistance.

Finally, I must give credit to my dear, sweet, kind, considerate, thoughtful, and wonderful husband, Roy. At times, he must have felt like a widower once again as I spent so many hours with my nose pressed up against my computer screen. His patient, loving support has allowed me to continue the process of sharing these delightful stories with others.

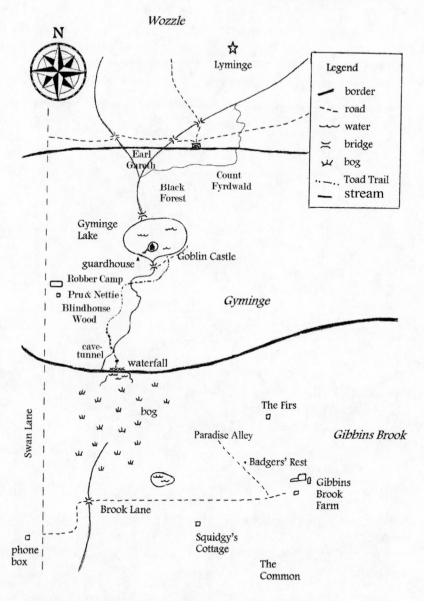

Wozzle and Gyminge, neighboring countries of Little People.
The Brook (or Common). Home for eleven of the Little People.

PRINCIPAL CHARACTERS

THE LITTLE PEOPLE / TWITH LOGUE
(TWI th LOW guh)

Jock	Leader of the Twith Logue
Jordy	Jock's roommate
Taymar	Jock's right-hand man
Gerald	Keeper of the Lore
Stumpy / Cleemo	Oldest of the Twith
Cymbeline (CYMBAL een)	Stumpy's niece
Barney	Stumpy's nephew, youngest of the Twith
Cydlo (SID low)	A woodcutter / King Rufus
Queen Sheba	His wife
Elisheba (Eh LISH eh buh)	His daughter / Princess Alicia
Dr. Vyruss Tyfuss	A new ally of the Twith
Ambro	Taymar's younger brother
Pru	An elderly lady in Gyminge
Nettie	Elisheba's nurse
Fyrdwald (FIRD walled)	Count of the Dark Forest

THE BEYONDERS

Gumpa	An early friend of the Twith
Gran'ma	His wife
Bimbo & Bollin	Their married sons / Shadow children
Stormy	An American girl
Bajjer (BAD jur)	Her brother
Specs	An English boy
Ginger	His sister
Uncle Andy	Gumpa's brother

Sarah & Peter	Andy's oldest daughter & her husband
Mike, Vickie, & Rosie	Their children
Julie & Max	Andy's youngest daughter & her husband
AJ & Jared	Grandsons from Texas
Titch	Granddaughter from Texas
Rachael & Micah	Grandchildren from Washington
Austin & Lucas	Brothers from Washington
Jenn & Nick	Grandchildren from Idaho
Gretchen and Katie	Sisters from Michigan
Ruthie, Margaret & Ellie	Shadow children

THE BIRDS AND ANIMALS

Buffo	The toad doorkeeper for the Twith
Bingo	Buffo's nephew
Blackie	The leader of the rabbits
Crusty	The eagle
Lupus	Cydlo's wolf-dog
Maggie	The magpie
Sparky	The sparrow
Tuwhit (Too WHIT)	The barn owl

THE WIZARD AND HIS CRONIES

Griswold (GRIZ walled)	The wizard
Rasputin (Rass PUH tin)	The wizard's raven
King Haymun	The king of the goblins
Jacko	The ferret
MoleKing	The king of the moles / Moley
Mrs. Griselda Squidge	The old woman on the Brook / Squidgy
Cajjer (CAD jur)	Squidgy's cat
The SnuggleWump	Squidgy's watch guard
The Teros	Titchy pterodactyls

PLACES

Gyminge (GIH minge)	Land of the Little People
Wozzle (WOZ el)	The kingdom of the wizard

DAYKO'S RIME

Forget not the land that you leave
As you flee from the pain and grief.
Let Truth in your heart ever burn.
It alone can bring your Return.

The hour the Return shall begin,
The captive shall tug at her chain.
Two spheres of night only you stay;
You shall not have longer a day.

From the water the shield will come,
The sword will come forth from the stone,
The dirk from the dust will return,
And the cloth will give up the crown.

The open door's better to guard
Than one which is bolted and barred.
Though conspire the foe and his friend
Yet the dog shall win in the end.

You go through the heart of the log,
Though the way is hid in the bog.
Black and white the flag high will rise.
The Child shall lead on to the Prize.

The goblet holds no draught of wine
And yields but a drop at a time.
The king will arise in the wood.
The Rime is at last understood.

The armour the flame will withstand.
Salt wind shall blow over the land
For light in the heart of the ring
Shall end the restraint of the king.

The belt is restored from the fire.
Brides shall process to the byre.
The loss of the Lore gives grief,
Though what is that to a life?

The fall will lead straight to the wall.
Hope is restored last of all.
Two reds in the night shall be green.
All's done. I've told what I've seen.

PREFACE

Gumpa loved to tell stories to children. It gave him a chance to be a child again himself. The *Twith Logue Chronicles*, which just means "Little People Stories," are fanciful, imaginative fairy tales that he told over a period of more than fifty years to children from ages five to fifteen. He just made them up as he went along, and the children always wanted to hear more. They would ask, "Will you please read some more out of your head?" When Gumpa retired, there weren't so many children around, so he began writing the stories.

The stories are a mixture of reality and fantasy, and sometimes it is hard to tell where one leaves off and the other begins. I think that sometimes he didn't even know himself. He always claimed that when he was a young boy in Cornwall, he actually met Taymar. The reality part is the old Tudor farmhouse and the surrounding area known as Gibbins Brook in Kent, England. The fantasy part is the Little People only half a thumb high. The adventures they have with Gumpa are where reality fades into fantasy.

The villain in this story learned how to do magic as a boy and grew up to become a mean, nasty wizard. Because anyone who uses magic develops The Magician's Twitch, Griswold has a twitchy right eye. That has foiled the perfect execution of more than one superior plan conceived by his brilliant but twisted mind. He is a bully at heart, very cunning and quite ruthless. He is also conceited.

The heroes are the Little People known as the Twith Logue or just plain Twith. They are far older than the English and have their origins in myth. These tiny folk are very wise and know many things we don't. They have senses we don't have so they can understand and talk to animals and birds. They do not use magic, and they *always tell the truth*. They know how to halt time so they can stop growing older whenever they want. Barney, the youngest among them, has chosen to stay a boy of ten. Even though they are only half a thumb high, they have managed to survive for many centuries. Winning battles doesn't always depend on how big you are. These wee folk live in the east of England in the kingdoms of Gyminge and Wozzle, tiny lands just on the northern edge of Gibbins Brook and separated from it by a bog. The bog, along with the meadows and wooded common land surrounding it, is known locally as the Brook.

The wicked wizard learned about the Little People and felt they would know the cure for his twitch. He decided to invade their countries and become their ruler. By the magic that he learned a thousand years ago in Cornwall, he made himself small and conquered first Wozzle and then Gyminge. Many of the Little People refused to be his subjects, so he sealed them up in bottles and stacked them in rows in the castle dungeons. The others he turned into goblins who serve in his army.

Seven of the Little People were able to escape with their valuable Book of Lore. It contains all the wisdom the Little People have acquired over the centuries. Because the wizard put an invisible curtain around the land, they could not return to Gyminge, and they settled on the Brook among the Beyonders. The people who live outside the land of the Little People are called Beyonders. The adults and children you know are all Beyonders. Very few Beyonders know about the Little People, so you are privileged to be learning about them.

Now picture yourself sitting on Gumpa's knee or gathered with other children at his feet and listen as Gumpa puts you into the world of the Little People, challenging you to tell the truth and taking you into strange and exciting adventures.

PROLOGUE

For centuries the wizard has been trying to capture the Twith who escaped so he can get hold of their Book of Lore. He is convinced that it contains the cure for The Magician's Twitch.

Mrs. Squidge, an old woman from Cornwall, came to the Brook to ask the wizard's help with her magic. It sometimes goes wrong. Squidgy made yeast buns that transformed a lizard into a dragon-like creature with two heads that she calls a SnuggleWump. The day Mrs. Squidge arrived, she met two of the Little People. Unable to get to the wizard because of the curtain, she wrote him a letter and mentioned she had met them.

The wizard was delighted to know where to find those who had escaped. Now he makes frequent excursions into the Beyond, attempting to capture them. On those occasions, he goes through a secret opening in the curtain. Once outside of Gyminge, he becomes a normal-sized man and changes back to Little People size when he returns.

The wizard has already made several attacks on the seven Little People. To begin with, he captured Stumpy, the oldest of the Twith. At the same time, a sneaky ferret stole the Shadow Book, which contains the shadows of children who helped in the past. Both the book and Stumpy were successfully recovered, but with the wizard closing in, the Twith decided to enlist the help of Beyonder children.

The children must *always tell the truth* or they will put the Little People in danger. The first four to arrive were Stormy and her brother, Bajjer, from America and Specs and his sister, Ginger, who are English. Children helping the Twith can become half a thumb high by holding the hand of one of the Little People. By crossing two fingers as the Little People hold their hand, the children resume their former stature. When the children are half a thumb high they can understand and talk to animals and birds, but until then they need an interpreter.

The wizard is a master of deceit and illusion. One reason he can be so sly and sneaky is that he has many disguises and can change from one creature to another very quickly. He can change himself into *almost* anything as long as it moves and has an eye that can twitch. In an attempt to obtain the Book of Lore, he changed himself into a dormouse and allowed himself to be wrapped up as a birthday gift. Bajjer was successful in throwing him out of Twith Mansion. However, the Twith realized the wizard would attack again and sent for a dozen more children. Five Shadow children were also called to come help.

In a cunning scheme to split the forces of the Little People in two, the wizard craftily changed himself into a delivery man. By tricking gran'ma into going outside with him, he captured her and took her to Goblin Castle. Once there, he chained her to the laundry room floor and made her iron goblin uniforms from dawn to dusk.

In over a thousand years, the Little People had never been able to penetrate the invisible curtain that the wizard erected around their homeland. But Buffo, the toad who acts as the Twith doorkeeper, showed them the way through a waterfall. Crusty, the golden eagle also found the way through by using the hole in the curtain that the wizard and his raven, Rasputin, use. Gran'ma was rescued along with a woodcutter, Cydlo, and his daughter, Elisheba. They are now part of the Twith family on the Brook.

Arriving just ahead of them were two other Twith. The goblin king, Haymun, who replaced King Rufus, chased his physician, Dr. Vyruss Tyfuss, onto the bog for attempting unauthorized surgery on the royal belly. Haymun was rescued by Rasputin, the wizard's raven, and carried to Squidgy's cottage. The good doctor was plucked from the bog by Crusty and taken to Twith Mansion. He made a promise to only speak truth and help the Twith regain their homeland.

While Jock, the little Scottish leader of the Twith, and his team were in Gyminge rescuing gran'ma, the wizard made an all-out attack on the farmhouse. His secret weapon was Squidgy's SnuggleWump. The children were ready for him and he was soundly defeated. No longer is the wizard clearly winning.

But the wizard does not accept defeat. He intends to get hold of the Book of Lore by hook or by crook!

The Twith know that one day they will be able to return to their homeland. Their ancient Seer, Dayko, left a cryptic poem called the Rime that reveals the events that must first take place. Gerald, who is the Keeper of the Lore, believes that he knows the exact day when the Return will be accomplished. However, there are still unfulfilled lines in Dayko's Rime that need to be resolved. Jock sent Bimbo and Bollin, the two Shadow brothers, into Gyminge on a secret quest. They returned with the Royal Shield and the Royal Sword, thus fulfilling two of the lines in Dayko's Rime. They also rescued Scayper, a Twith they met when they were put in the dungeon.

Many secrets were unveiled. To the amazement and joy of the Twith, Cydlo confessed that he is King Rufus, and his daughter, Elisheba, is Princess Alicia. Not only that, but in happier days long ago she was betrothed by her father to the oldest son of the Earl of Up-Horton, who is none other than Taymar, Jock's right-hand man.

Scayper surprised them twice. First, he revealed that he is Taymar's brother, Ambro. The other surprise was that Cymbeline, Stumpy's niece, is his long lost love. Both couples plan to be married on the farm, so gran'ma is busy making preparations for a double wedding.

The wizard returned to Gyminge to investigate rumors of invisible Chinese invaders. He expected his troops to arrive from the Brook to help. When they failed to do so and no invaders could be found, the wizard went back to Squidgy's cottage.

KENNETH G. OLD & PATTY OLD WEST

His attack on the farmhouse may have failed, but that did not stop his mischief. As he schemed how to trick the Twith, an opportunity presented itself with the arrival of a circus in the nearby village. He convinced the owner of the circus to give a performance on the Brook and used the occasion to steal the Book of Lore.

The Twith were devastated until they discovered that Gerald had created a pseudo book containing only a small portion of the actual Lore. The rest was Cornish recipes. The wizard was not amused.

Furious at being tricked himself, the wizard used Queen Sheba as a bargaining tool, offering to exchange her for the authentic Book of Lore. The Twith accepted the wizards offer, and as the exchange was about to take place, a ferret ran off with the Book of Lore. Amazingly, the wizard released the queen and went to negotiate with Jacko. Agreeing on a price, the ferret left to retrieve the Book of Lore.

The wizard waited and is still waiting for him to return.

Now let's continue the mystery, the excitement, and the adventures of the Little People.

RESIDENTS ON THE BROOK

There are four families who live at Gibbins Brook Farm on the Brook. They are all related. Gumpa and gran'ma live in the old farmhouse. One half is an old Tudor black-and-white timbered dwelling that was built before Columbus discovered America. The other half is a bit newer, built three-hundred years later and is red brick.

Gumpa has a brother, Andy, who lives with his wife in the building once used as a stable. Andy's oldest daughter and her husband live in the converted barn. They have three children: twelve-year-old Mike; Vickie, who is nine; and little three-year old Rosie. The cowshed is now comfortable living quarters for Andy's youngest daughter, Julie, and her family.

The children who were called to help in the battle with the wizard have been told they can call Gumpa's brother *Uncle* Andy. There are sixteen of them presently living in the farmhouse. All but six are grandchildren. They are all ready and waiting for the next adventure. What a summer this is proving to be for them! And Dayko foretold in his Rime that a Beyonder child will lead the Twith to victory in the Last Battle.

There are eleven Little People who live at Gibbins Brook Farm. The seven Twith who escaped from Gyminge on the back of Crusty, the golden eagle, decided to settle on the Brook. Until the old woman from Cornwall arrived on her broomstick, they lived in the middle of the Common in Smiler's cottage. Now they have an underground home built near the well of the farmhouse called Twith Mansion. Recently, four other Twith who managed to flee Gyminge have joined them.

After Gumpa and gran'ma moved to the farm, Stumpy and his family moved into the farmhouse. They have an apartment upstairs by the chimney that includes two bedrooms, a kitchen, and a workshop for Stumpy. He is the oldest of the Twith and shares a bedroom with his ten-year old nephew Barney. His niece Cymbeline used to be the only girl but happily now shares her bedroom with the new arrival from Gyminge, Elisheba.

The other seven Little People live in Twith Mansion. Jock shares his room with his long-time mountain climbing friend, Jordy. Taymar, the tallest of the Twith, shares a room with Gerald, who is the new High Seer. Ambro is in a small guest room, and Cydlo and his wife are in the large guest room.

There are also five Shadow children who are living in Twith Mansion for the summer. Jock collected their shadows many years ago, and Gerald put them into the Shadow Book. It is something like a photograph album but much more. Jock can call the shadows back off the page, and the children are the same age as when they helped in the past. They are not like other children, however. They come back half a thumb high, and they are weightless.

A short-term and increasingly frequent visitor to the mansion is the wizard's new ambassador, Dr. Vyruss Tyfuss. He was court physician to the goblin king, Haymun, who replaced King Rufus. Dr. Tyfuss was saved from drowning in the bog by Crusty and has become an ally of the Twith by promising to help them regain Gyminge. The wizard, not knowing that Vyruss has changed sides, appointed him the Ambassador of Gyminge to the Beyond. Ironically, he also admonished him to only tell the truth. Dr. Tyfuss now has a foot in both camps.

The other resident on the Brook is Squidgy, who came from Cornwall and moved into Smiler's cottage about thirty years ago. Her cottage is in the middle of the woods towards the southern end of the Common, and the wizard uses her residence as a base when he is on the Brook. Mrs. Squidge is always a little overawed at the presence in her humble home of the famous Wizard of Wozzle.

She has a licorice-swirl cat, Cajjer, who is very bad-tempered. He scratches and bites, sometimes without provocation. Cajjer has a shorter tail than the one he was born with or, for that matter, the one he arrived on the Brook with. It has suffered three different amputations. The first occurred when Jacko, the ferret, mistook him for a rabbit and bit a chunk off the end of his tail. The next came when Taymar whacked it with his Twith axe during the battle at the cottage to rescue Stumpy. And most recently, the goblin king, Haymun, tried to sever his tail entirely by chomping down on it with his teeth to keep from drowning in the waterfall pool.

Squidgy also has a creature she calls a SnuggleWump who guards her cottage. His creation was something of an accident when a lizard ate some of her yeast buns gone wrong. The animal looks like a dragon but is bigger and has two heads on long, sinuous necks. Each head has only one eye. The eyes change color from green to red when he is angry. Sometimes he pretends to be angry because it pleases his mistress. Each head used to have two ears, but they now only have one each. They were lost in two different battles with the Twith.

There are six titchy teros perched on the ridge of her cottage. These creatures were once chickens raised by Uncle Andy's son-in-law Max. Unfortunately, they consumed crumbs from another batch of yeast buns gone wrong. They, like the SnuggleWump, have great affection for their creator.

Another odd creature was created from that same batch of yeast buns. Moley, the king of the moles, gobbled down several and transformed into a zebra-striped duckbilled platypus that the wizard calls a Zebrotter. Griswold trained him to be a weightlifter, and the animal has gone off with the circus as the Masked Menace from Madagascar.

The Twith intend, come-what-may, to return home this summer and see the king restored to his throne. They will rescue their family and friends from their long captivity in bottles in the dungeons of Gyminge and Wozzle. According to the Rime of the ancient seer, Dayko, only five weeks are available after the weddings for the Return to take place. They must complete all their unfinished tasks and defeat the wizard by August twelfth. Otherwise, they will miss their first opportunity in over a thousand years to return to Gyminge. Dayko's Rime has set the clock ticking, so the numbering of days is very important!

THE QUEEN BEGINS
HER STORY

It has been a few hours only since Queen Sheba stepped through the curtain from Gyminge onto the Brook. The wizard actually pushed her through even though he did not have the Book of Lore in his possession as per the agreement. The exchange was to be simultaneous, but Jacko tore through like a tornado and snatched the precious package out from under the nose of the wizard. Tuwhit, the owl, quickly took Jock, Jordy, Taymar, and Barney to search for the ferret.

The surprise release of the queen makes this a special night. The children and grownups alike celebrate with continuous singing and dancing on the fireplace hearth in the long room of the farmhouse. There is a lull in the action when the four searchers arrive back. They couldn't find the ferret, but in an unexpected chain of events, they recovered the stolen Book of Lore. The celebrating resumes with even more enthusiasm.

Downstairs in Twith Mansion, Gerald is concerned about having both the Book of Lore and the queen. He summons Jock and Cydlo down to Twith Mansion to discuss the matter. The queen wants to listen in.

The new High Seer is worried. "We need to discuss the agreement we made with the wizard for the exchange of the Book of Lore for the queen. Now that we have the queen, it is not honest to retain the book. By doing so, we are not keeping to our side of the agreement. The slightest slip from truth could prevent our return to Gyminge. That will mean an end to attaining our goal of recovering our homeland."

Queen Sheba breaks in. "I will gladly return to Gyminge so you can keep the Book of Lore. I won't mind being put back in a bottle, because I know it won't be long before you will be there to rescue me."

Gerald is firm. "No, that won't resolve the problem. Our agreement was that the wizard would receive the authentic Book of Lore and that is what we must keep to."

Cydlo agrees. "Yes, you are right Gerald. Please go get Vyruss. He must leave right away to get the Book of Lore into the wizard's hands."

Gerald interrupts Vyruss in the middle of dancing with Stormy. The doctor is reluctant to leave but realizes how important it is for the Twith to keep their word.

Gerald has the authentic Book of Lore all wrapped and ready to go. He places it in a small satchel and hands it to Dr. Tyfuss. "Come. Tuwhit is waiting outside to take you as far as the croc' pond."

Jock and Gerald accompany the doctor to the croc' pond where Buffo will take him to the waterfall. After dropping Vyruss off, Jock has the owl take them for a spin around the Brook to be certain no suspicious activity is taking place.

Gran'ma brings a temporary halt to the festivities by announcing, "It will soon be time for devotions and a bedtime story for the children. Instead of a story tonight, we will hear some of Queen Sheba's story. But it will be off to bed for everyone by nine o'clock!"

As far as gran'ma is concerned, whether or not it is as bright as noonday outside, nine o'clock is the time intended from the beginning of time for good people of any age to be in bed and fast asleep.

The activities begin winding down. The music ceases and the instruments are put away. Sizes for all the Beyonders are adjusted upwards. Vickie quickly runs over and gets her grandfather so he can listen to the queen's story too. All the children except her brother, Mike, scurry upstairs to put on their pajamas, clean their teeth, and get back downstairs for devotions. They are anticipating a very special story from the queen! Most of the children choose to be shrunk once more, and Barney is happy to oblige. Jock and Gerald are back from their trip around the Brook. They didn't observe anything out of the ordinary.

The tallest of the large inlaid Indian tables is covered with a red cloth. Chairs have been brought up from below, and Cydlo and the queen are seated on them. They are at one end of the table, looking out towards the room. On the same table, resting on cushions or against each other, are almost thirty little folk facing them. There are the five Shadow children, the seven original Twith plus the two younger arrivals, and sixteen of the twenty-one Beyonders gathered to listen.

The only two children not present are Specs and Bajjer. Backed up by Crusty and Cydlo's wolf-dog, Lupus, they volunteered to be the outside patrol. Both have alarm whistles in case they should be needed.

Stormy tells her brother, "I promise to remember every word and not forget a single bit of what the queen has to say. I have a tablet and I'll make a lot of notes." Only she and Vickie among the children have stayed Beyonder-size. Vickie is snuggled against her grandfather on the settee while Gumpa and gran'ma are in their usual wing-backed chairs either side of the fireplace. Stormy is curled comfortably at gran'ma's feet. All are settled and waiting anxiously for the queen to begin.

Gran'ma has taken the queen into her heart as a daughter. She quietly tells her, "You will need to speak up loudly and clearly so everyone can hear. It shouldn't be any real problem. We Beyonders manage all right with the other Twith, and we had no difficulty when Elisheba told her story. Please don't miss out any details. You won't be able to finish your story at one telling, but that's all right. We'll find time later. Cydlo and Elisheba had to spread their telling over several sessions."

The queen looks around and receives nods from Jock and gran'ma. Her husband and daughter smile approvingly. She takes a deep breath and begins, "I need to start before the invasion of Gyminge took place. King Rufus, Alicia, and I lived at Gyminge Castle on the edge of the lake.

"Before the king left the castle to go north on an errand to the Dark Forest, we secretly sent our daughter into hiding in Blindhouse Wood. Nettie had been her nurse throughout her growing years and was sent with her. We kept a small cottage in the woods that we occasionally used when we went among the people as though we ourselves were peasants. To avoid drawing attention to her, there were no guards at the cottage, and they had no servants. We agreed that direct contact would be infrequent, but courier birds brought us news on a daily basis. In those days, Gyminge had plenty of birds, but they all managed to flee before the wizard could finish putting his curtain around the land.

"King Rufus was meeting with his two good friends, Earl Gareth and Count Fyrdwald. Earl Gareth, the father of Taymar and Ambro, reported on events at the north border. The news was not good. An invasion from Wozzle was imminent. It was unlikely that our country could withstand the forces about to be unleashed against it. Wozzle was fully mobilized for war.

"The king returned in haste and wanted me to go fetch Alicia and seek refuge in the Beyond. Birds would take us to King Druthan in Cornwall who could be relied upon to help. I told my husband firmly that I would stay with him come-what-may. I did not marry him in order to run away when trouble brewed. He knew better than to argue with me." She smiles sweetly at her husband, who squeezes her hand.

"Then he told me of private discussions he had with Earl Gareth about the matter we often discussed between ourselves. Who would be the most suitable husband for our lovely daughter? Of all the young men in Gyminge or in Wozzle, we agreed that the oldest son of the Earl of Up-Horton would be our choice. The Earl and he agreed upon the match and exchanged their own rings as a binding pledge to each other. Alicia was now betrothed to Taymar."

Elisheba turns her eyes towards Taymar who smiles and pats her hand.

"In view of the expected attack from Wozzle, there could be no delay in informing Alicia of her betrothal. We couldn't be certain that we ourselves would survive the fighting. I needed to leave as soon as possible to go tell Elisheba the good news. I would give her the pledge ring and tell her she was bound by the ring to Taymar as long as they lived. After that, I was to act at my own discretion, but I had no doubt in my mind what that would be. I would return at once to my husband.

"I hastened to get ready and selected plain, inconspicuous clothing. I tied my hair back in the style of a peasant woman. After some thought, I removed all my rings, including my wedding ring, and gave them to my husband for safekeeping. We agreed it was wise to remove all identification. I tied the betrothal ring in my handkerchief and hid the handkerchief securely deep in my clothing.

"The king checked the horses and used two of them as pack animals loaded with long-term supplies for the cottage. Only two men, good soldiers but clad as peasants, accompanied me as my escort. We traveled as a peasant family returning home after shopping in the town. We did not expect trouble in the land to the south. The king, also clad inconspicuously, traveled with me for a short distance before returning to the castle to consult with Dayko, the High Seer. The look at his back as he galloped away was the last I saw of my husband until this afternoon here on the Brook."

Gran'ma senses the anguish in the queen's heart and glances over at Gumpa. *I'm thankful I was only separated from him for a week. I don't think I could bear a longer length of time away from him.*

The queen continues, "We proceeded on our way into the woods. As we passed through a clearing on the far side of the stream, we were suddenly attacked by five or six armed men on horseback. They came at us from both front and behind, shouting wildly. It scared the horses, and they reared on their hind legs. Arrows whistled through the air. They missed my men, but both their horses were hit. The gang of attackers and my own two guards were soon engaged in close-up sword fighting on horseback. First one and then the other of my men was unseated. The bodies of my two guards were sprawled on the ground. They were good and loyal men who died trying to save me."

There is an indrawn gasp from her listeners. They are right there with her. This is the very worst thing that could happen.

The queen brushes away the tears that come from remembering her fallen companions. "The robbers seemed to ignore me. I thought that perhaps they were after the supplies on the packhorses and would not pursue a simple village woman. I did not dare to head for the cottage. That would betray the location of my daughter. I spied a narrow path to the west and spurred my horse along it.

"I grew up with horses and am a good horsewoman. I had no trouble leaping the brook, but the recent rain proved to be my undoing. My horse slipped and fell, and I was unseated. The leader of the gang was a huge man with a body like an ox. He had a head of long, thick, black hair and an untidy black beard. Blackbeard himself was upon me and grabbed me by the shoulders in a grip that left me sore for days. I was devastated. My errand had ended in disaster. I was a captive of robbers and no one knew where I was."

There is absolute silence. No one stirs and no one fidgets. All are hanging on her every word. Stormy has filled six pages of her tablet with notes. Listening most carefully of all among the tiny folk on the table are Elisheba, Ambro, Bimbo, and Bollin. They each had their own encounters with Blackbeard and are reliving their own experiences. Unknown to the queen, those experiences with Hardrada have already been shared with the others in the room. They, too, know how dangerous the man is.

BEDTIME

Suddenly the familiar Westminster chimes begin striking the hours. The expulsion of breath from the children is like multiple balloons deflating. Dismayed faces turn to look at the clock. Everyone counts silently as the clock strikes nine times. The children want a miracle, but there is little hope that it will happen. Time only moved backwards once before in all of history when the prophet Isaiah asked for the shadow on the staircase to move backwards rather than forwards. It isn't very likely it is going to happen right now. No heads turn to look towards the staircase. That points up to bed.

No one moves. Cydlo and the queen are holding hands but not looking as though they need to do something. Jock makes no move, and neither does Gerald. The children are certain they know what the real name of Blackbeard is, and they are desperate to know what is going to happen to the queen now. Taymar and Ambro are holding the hands of their future brides and quite content to wait until morning for the outcome.

Gran'ma sighs. *The queen has hardly begun to tell her story. This is the last available evening before the wedding celebrations get under way. Tomorrow evening is the rehearsal dinner, and the weddings themselves are the following day.* She looks across at the little table packed with Little People and Twith-size children.

Her thoughts are uneasy. *Fourteen of them are the Beyonder children. This is what we promised them when we invited them to come to the Brook for the summer. We advertised, 'Do things you have never done before, see things you have never dreamed of, learn things never written in books. The children will be greatly enlarged by their experiences.' This is a precious moment, and there are some experiences that should not be cut short.* Her shoulders sag and she looks across at Gumpa wistfully.

KENNETH G. OLD & PATTY OLD WEST

Gumpa doesn't need words from gran'ma to understand what she is thinking. This happens with married couples. They talk to each other without voicing words. He can read her thoughts, *Gumpa, help me. What do we do now?*

He thinks about bedtime deadlines. *Deadlines have their uses. They are rules by which people develop ordered, balanced, rested lives. Children need more time in bed than grownups and should go to bed earlier than grownups. If children burn the candle at both ends, they get grumpy and are much more likely to catch chickenpox, break the best china, or trip over the dog. It's nine o'clock now and time for bed.*

The children know that Gumpa likes to be in bed by nine o'clock himself and wait anxiously for him to speak.

Gumpa isn't finished thinking things through. *However, a set time for going to bed is not a monument like the Sphinx or the Washington Monument or a fixed date in history like 1066 or July Fourth. Bedtime needs to be flexible. If an eclipse of the moon will occur at ten o'clock, then the children have a right to see the moon disappear into blackness as the earth sails across, blocking the light from the sun. Even if it is after bedtime.*

Most of the grandchildren are wondering, *What is taking Gumpa so long to say, "Off to bed, children."*

Gumpa is considering all the options. *There are times when the best of rules, such as always going to Sunday school, need to be set aside because that is the very time Great Aunt Bertha from Australia is going to visit. I'm not quite sure that is a good enough reason to miss Sunday school. It's a good thing I'm not sharing my thoughts with anyone else.*

Furthermore, from remarks gran'ma made while we were having early-morning tea, I'm aware that the dressmaking for the wedding has fallen behind schedule and a little more time would be welcome. Not only that, but she would like time to make a new dress for the queen to wear to her daughter's wedding. Otherwise, she'll be wearing a secondhand one from someone the same size. Surprisingly, this

38

last thought is Gumpa's own fresh idea and not something he gathered from gran'ma.

He has made his decision. In his most decisive voice he says, "Nine o'clock. That's the time for bed, children."

The children all wear sad expressions as though they will burst into tears at any moment. No one moves. Not even Uncle Andy.

Gumpa looks around, draws a deep breath, and continues. "I have a suggestion to make to Cydlo. I haven't discussed this with gran'ma but..."

Specs thinks. *That's superfluous. Everyone knows he hasn't discussed it with gran'ma. Neither of them has said a single word to the other since the queen started telling her story. Carry on, Gumpa.*

"This is a very important moment. Cydlo and Queen Sheba have just been reunited after a very long time of being apart. Furthermore, Elisheba needs to find out what happened to her mother and so do the rest of us. With the upcoming weddings, it is difficult to see where and when we are going to get together again to hear the rest of the story before the Return. In fact, it may not be possible. That would be very sad. Now perhaps the queen is too tired to continue."

The queen smiles and shakes her head vigorously.

"Well, if she is not, then I would suggest that we put off bedtime until Queen Sheba has completed her story."

It is too soon for the children to break out with clapping and applause, but they are ready to *Whoopee* at a flicker of a chance to be noisy. They'll wait a while. The suggestion has yet to be approved.

Gumpa continues. "We shall need to make certain adjustments if this is what we do. Breakfast tomorrow will not be until nine o'clock, and none of the children must stir until they have had a full eight and a half hours in bed.

"Furthermore, I would suggest that to compensate for our late night, the weddings themselves should be put off from Friday evening until the same time Saturday evening or even Sunday

KENNETH G. OLD & PATTY OLD WEST

evening. I can see one or two possible benefits from this suggestion. It will give gran'ma extra time to complete preparations for the weddings, and I am sure the choirs will appreciate extra time to practice. There shouldn't be too much trouble notifying our bird and animal guests.

"I do realize this affects the time available to complete the Return, but plans need to be flexible, and unforeseen events have happened in the last day or so. But you, Cydlo, have the larger picture and you will need to decide. What are your thoughts?"

Cydlo does indeed have the larger picture. "The wizard is at Mrs. Squidge's cottage negotiating with Jacko for a document the ferret does not possess. However, somewhere in Gyminge near the southern border, Ambassador Tyfuss waits to deliver the Book of Lore to the wizard. Once he gets that and reads it through, the Twith will be dealing with a completely new situation—one we have not previously encountered.

"By August twelfth the complete campaign to recover Gyminge and Wozzle must be over. We could end up with time to spare, but on the other hand, we could be out of time completely. In that case, each day counts."

Cymbeline is whispering to Ambro, and they are both stirring, ready to spring to their feet. Cydlo takes the hint from their shuffling. He caught a hint of their whispers. "Perhaps if Ambro and Cymbeline would organize some hot cocoa, then we could take time until that is ready to stretch ourselves. I think your suggestion is a good one, Gumpa. Provided gran'ma, the two young couples, Gerald, and Jock also agree, let us complete the queen's story now and put off the weddings for twenty-four hours until Saturday evening."

Stormy and gran'ma are already on their way to the kitchen as the applause breaks out. Hot cocoa sounds good to them too. If there is disagreement from anyone, it would not be possible to hear it.

THE QUEEN'S
STORY CONTINUES

The children know they are on borrowed time. They are as quiet as mice in a pantry. Specs and Bajjer are on guard duty outside. Gumpa asks two of his grandsons from Washington, "Austin and Lucas, will you go replace Specs and Bajjer so they have a chance to listen first-hand?" The boys are always willing to be helpful and head outside. The two arrivals are quickly filled in on what has happened so far.

The queen takes up her story again. "I had a hope that my horse might break free and find its way back to its stable, but Blackbeard grabbed the reins before it had a chance to bolt. He held me by my hair as he remounted. Then he grabbed my arms and swung me up in front of him. He did not recognize me as the queen.

"Blackbeard had the horses walk slowly back to where they lived. Two of the men and three of the horses had been injured, so those three riders were on foot. The six men in the gang were ill-clad and frightening in appearance. Blackbeard, in a rollicking good mood, was at the head of the column. As he got closer to home, he broke into song with his men joining in. I wondered what they would do to me.

"We followed the same little path to the west that I tried to use to escape. We traveled westwards for several hours, crossing over several of the main north-south paths that I recognized through Blindhouse Wood. We traveled such a long distance that it seemed we would surely reach the edge of the forest and soon break through into open country. Before we did, a small side path northwards by a stream took us into an encampment in a clearing. It was clearly the robber's home.

"As we rode in, women and children ran out of small, roughly made homes around the edge of the clearing. Blackbeard swung me off the horse and set me down on the ground. He rode off towards the stable. The women were curious and gathered around me. I did not want to be recognized and lowered my head, but it was no good. They shouted, 'She is the queen!' 'Yes! It is the queen!' There was no animosity, rather surprise, almost awe. They reached out and touched my clothes, my hands, my hair. One woman brought me a drink of milk, and another gave me a chair to sit on.

"Blackbeard was there at once. 'Are you sure?' He peered closely into my face. 'Are you sure?' The women were sure. There was no chance of secrecy now. Seizing my hands, he looked at my fingers, clearly not the hands of a peasant woman. I was grateful I removed my rings before I left, but my fingers showed the marks where they had been.

"He gave instructions. 'You two, take her into the prisoners' hut and search her thoroughly. Bring anything you find to me. If she's the queen, she's going to make us rich. Are you the queen?' I answered, 'Do I look like a queen?'

"The women bustled me away. They searched me thoroughly but not roughly. All they found was a purse of small coins and my handkerchief with the betrothal ring tied in one corner. When they undid the knot and found the ring, they got really excited. They knew Hardrada would be interested in that. My handkerchief was embroidered with my initials. That was a mistake I regretted. I hoped they would not notice and I asked if I could please keep my handkerchief. They discussed it and decided Blackbeard would have no use for it. I breathed a sigh of relief. I didn't want him knowing for certain that I was the queen, When he questioned me, he would surely ask where the queen was going in disguise with such a light escort. It would not take much for him to search the path beyond where he attacked us and find Alicia and Nettie. That must never happen.

"From the women's conversation, I learned that Blackbeard's real name was Hardrada. He took the name from an eleventh-century Norwegian king who was so called because he was a Hard-Ruler. Everyone in the camp was afraid of him. There was a tree house in an oak tree on the west edge of the clearing and that was his home.

"He was unmarried, and the women provided him with meals in rotation when there was no communal cookhouse in use. The wives asked if I could cook. They hoped that by having a female prisoner, he would restart the cookhouse with me as the cook.

"The women didn't tie me up, and I was grateful to them for that. They took what they found on me and left me in the empty prisoners' hut. As they pulled the door closed, they left it slightly ajar to allow a slice of light into the darkness. I was grateful because there were no windows.

"One of the women returned with a message from Hardrada. If I promised not to try to escape, he would allow me to live in the unused cookhouse. I thought about the alternative if I did not agree and shuddered.

"When I agreed, the woman led me across the clearing to a wooden log building at the foot of Hardrada's tree house. She brought me a bed and bedding from her own home. I asked her what was going to happen to me. She smiled. 'You're one of the lucky ones. You have a good chance of getting out of here, not like the rest of us. I imagine in your case it will be for ransom. You'll just have to wait and see.'

"In the following days, there were many comings and goings at the camp, but Hardrada himself did not leave. I wasn't asked to do any cooking, but I did clean the cookhouse thoroughly. With the sacks of flour and fresh vegetables from the garden, I was able to prepare bread and soups for myself. I stayed inside the cookhouse and didn't venture outside. The women stopped by occasionally to drop off fruit and vegetables and inquire whether there was anything I needed. They were kind to me and seemed to be victims themselves. They must have told their children to stay away, for they never came near.

"I gathered the men were planning a new raid in the area where I was captured, but the women had no details other than that the men expected to be away all day and they would go on horseback rather than on foot.

"One morning I was called to Hardrada's house. He was in a good mood. He told me to sit down and asked me about the ring I was carrying. I answered that it belonged to a friend. He did not question me further, nor did he show me that he still had the ring. He asked me where the king was. I told him he was at Gyminge Castle. He then asked me about the errand that I was on, but I did not answer and he gave up questioning.

"He told me that I would be returned to Gyminge Castle. A satisfactory ransom had been agreed. Three of his men would escort me. He meant no offense, but he could not spare more than that. Unfortunately, he himself had other engagements. He asked if I could be ready to leave within one hour. He trusted that the arrangements for my stay were satisfactory and that I had no complaints.

"I was delighted to be going home to my husband and had nothing to say to Hardrada. I wanted to ask him about what was happening with the Wozzle invasion scare but doubted that he would tell the truth. I could wait for a few more hours and find out for myself.

"The men who escorted me took two spare horses with side panniers. Hardrada instructed them about the hand-over. 'You see,' he said, 'this is not the first time I have exchanged a captive for a ransom.'

"He made it clear that at the end of our journey the leader of my own robber escort would be a hundred paces ahead. He would first meet the escort that would be waiting to take me to the castle. The remainder of us would wait back. The men from the castle would have their own animals fully loaded with the ransom.

When Hardrada's man was satisfied there was no trickery, the exchange would be made and I would be on my way home.

"I was worried for my husband and more so for Alicia. Could Hardrada's errand today be to search for her? Even so, my heart was singing as I mounted my horse and turned back to wave to the women and children in the clearing."

The Queen Concludes
Her Story

The queen smiles at her audience, who are listening attentively to every word. "We were not more than an hour on our journey when we were overtaken by Hardrada and his party of five men riding hard. I recognized they were a raiding party out for trouble, and I was fearful for whoever stood in their way. I hoped desperately that it would not prove to be Alicia and Nettie. I questioned my escort where Hardrada was bound, but they knew nothing.

"When our path crossed one of the main north-south trails through Blindhouse Wood, we turned north. There were travelers on this path, but as we passed them, they averted their gaze away from us. The robber band was obviously well-known in those parts. It was safer for the traveler to see nothing, do nothing, remember nothing, and have nothing.

"As we approached the north end of the forest, our leader indicated for us to stop. He galloped ahead, taking with him the two pannier horses. The horses grazed as we waited. Suddenly our man was silhouetted in the opening among the trees, beckoning us to join him. I was filled with joy, expecting to gallop out into the comforting welcome of my husband's arms. He would surely come to meet me.

"It was not so. We were met by an escort of a dozen goblin cavalry carrying lances with black flags. I was completely devastated as I saw that a black flag, not the Royal Flag, was flying from the castle turret. Before I could wheel my horse back into the woods or react in any way, I was surrounded."

A series of soft groans echo around the room.

"In that awful moment of total despair, I knew at once that all was lost. My husband was probably dead, I would never see my daughter again, and I was a prisoner of the Wizard of Wozzle. Hardrada negotiated my exchange with the castle but not with my husband. The various treasures from the castle for which I was being bartered were being transferred from the cavalry horses into the panniers as quickly as possible. However, the escort to take me to the castle did not wait for that to be completed.

"We cantered slowly down the hill. Surrounded on all sides, I had no opportunity to break away. Goblin soldiers were everywhere. We passed many of our own people trudging on foot towards the open parade ground before the castle. Just a few days earlier there would have been hurrahs when I was seen, but now there was only silence and the sense of a terrible oppression. I knew I was recognized, but people looked up without curiosity. Their spirits were broken, and it was easy to observe they had lost all hope. How had we been broken so soon?

"As we approached the main entrance, I saw that the wooden bridge to Dayko's house had been burned down. We clattered under the portcullis into the castle courtyard. I was assisted to dismount. I resolved to behave as a queen should behave and not show how frightened I was. I looked for an opportunity to ask someone I recognized for news of the king, but I saw no one. The faces were all strangers. The entire castle staff had been replaced.

"I was led up the steps into the great reception hall. There, sitting on my husband's throne as though he had every right to be there, was the Wizard of Wozzle. This was the first time I had seen him, but I knew at once who he was. He rose as I entered, came down the steps towards me, and gave me a slight bow of greeting. Gently, he guided me towards a small table set for tea. Although he had a triumphant sneer on his face, he spoke kindly. 'Queen Sheba, I believe. My greetings. Welcome home. Join me for tea.'

"He politely seated me and poured the tea. 'Before we talk about your future, do you have any questions for me?'

"I asked him where my husband and daughter were and what he had done with them.

"He replied, 'If I could be certain in my answer, I would tell you. It seems likely they are both dead. However, my inquiries are not yet fully complete. I realize this is sad news for you.'

"I could hardly refrain from bursting into tears, but I stiffened myself. He would not see me cry. I asked what he was going to do with me.

"He smiled. 'Ma'am, I have appointed one of your seers as king in your husband's place. His name is Haymun, and he says that you know him. He is unmarried and you, I presume, are now a widow. After a suitable period of mourning for the late king, I am sure the new king would be delighted to make a proposal of marriage. That would secure the lifestyle to which you are accustomed. I would happily concur with such an arrangement. I hope that you can agree. In the event that you should find his proposal unattractive, I will find it necessary to place you in storage. We have many of your nobles and gentry in storage already. Our dungeons are very full, so I hope you will consider things carefully and not force me to this action.'

"I was relieved to hear that he did not intend to kill me. I had little appetite for the refreshments on offer, but I nibbled at a scone and sipped some tea. He was not surprised but looked saddened by my emphatic refusal to consider retaining my position by marrying the usurper to my husband's throne.

"He did not publicly humiliate me during the bottling process, which followed quickly afterwards. It was done in the castle courtyard, but the gates were closed. Only a few soldiers were present. There was no particular ceremony, although I observed the wizard watching from the upper balcony.

"The bottle was the center of attention just as a gallows would be at a hanging. Six soldiers were appointed to place me inside as smoothly and quickly as possible. It was a rectangular-shaped bottle, not round, and it laid flat with its mouth towards me. I faced away from the bottle and was told to lie face down. The men had a lot of experience in bottling people. They had probably done it hundreds of times in the past few weeks. I wasn't bound but had to place my hands behind my back. I was lifted face down, and my feet inserted into the bottle.

"Then they slid me further into the bottle. I could only see the boots of the soldiers pushing me. The bottle was lifted upright so the rest of my body slid in until I was completely within the bottle. When my feet touched the bottom, I adjusted my balance to stand as well as I was able. There was little spare space, and I could hardly move.

"The wooden plug to seal the bottle was inserted and knocked in tight. I smelled a whiff of candle grease. A full ladle of smoking candle wax was poured on the top of the bottle plug. Fortunately for me, no hot grease came inside the bottle. I must have fainted, for that was all I remembered until the day before yesterday."

The children's imaginations are working overtime picturing the bottling process. Ambro was taken captive and bottled himself. He remembers his own experiences. For both of them, it worked out well in the end. But it was many centuries between bottling and freedom. He gives Cymbeline's hand a grateful, loving squeeze.

"That day I awoke to the voice of the wizard calling, 'Wake up! Wake up!' I was still in the bottle, and he and another man pulled me out. I had no idea where I was, but it proved to be the formal sitting room of our apartments in Gyminge Castle. There was little change in the appearance of the wizard. The young man with him introduced himself as Dr. Vyruss Tyfuss, the Ambassador of Gyminge to the Beyond. The wizard informed me this particular young man told the truth. I was given an opportunity to freshen myself up. While I was doing that, my bottle was replaced in the secret hideaway room behind the fireplace.

"The wizard told me that many years had passed and times were very different now. Although he still believed that my daughter had drowned in the lake, he had just discovered that it was likely my husband was still alive. He informed me that Dr. Tyfuss was going on a mission to the Beyond to this very farmhouse. I was told that I could send a personal letter if I wished.

"I see now that it was all part of the wizard's plans to get hold of the Book of Lore. But it gave me the opportunity to be reunited with my family, so I am grateful that events happened the way they did.

"The rest of the story you already know. When the ferret stole the Book of Lore, I was certain that the exchange had failed. Imagine my surprise when the wizard told me to go forward and gave me a push! Now I'm the one who has a great deal of catching up to do."

Gran'ma takes her cue. "Thank you, Queen Sheba, for your story. You will perhaps want to continue your conversations, but if we are to have breakfast at nine o'clock, a good number of us need to head off for bed. Goodnight, everyone."

There is a chorus of goodnights. Hugs and kisses for the ones who are not too grown up not to want a proper child's goodnight. Morning will soon be here.

Cydlo and the queen remain for a while as the Beyonders troop upstairs. He looks at her with admiration for her courage. "I never knew that Hardrada bartered you for ransom. That was what condemned us to separation for centuries. I was in constant fear during the intervening years that I would never see you again, my beloved. One day, if Hardrada is still alive, there is going to be a fierce and bitter reckoning between us. And that goes for the wizard as well."

THE WIZARD GOES HOME

At Squidgy's cottage, only Mrs. Squidge has retired to bed. Her occasional groans go through her closed and bolted bedroom door into the living room down below. She just aches all over from her early morning collision in midair with Rasputin and his passenger. When Cajjer fell off the broomstick, it careened wildly and gave her a good whack on the head. The raven's beak then pierced both hands, and she had great difficulty steering the broom back home.

Cajjer crash-landed in the croc' pond and barely avoided drowning. Both are battered and bruised and the cat is hiding under her bed, doing his best not to whine. He does not wish to be thrown out of the bedroom or, even worse, farther outside onto the porch. His head is thumping like a steam train chugging up a steep gradient because of banging it on the front door in his race to get back into the cottage. He reminds himself, "In the future, I shall check that the door is open before trying to get through it using my head as a battering ram. Either that or take to wearing a crash helmet."

In the living room, the wizard waits. He and Jacko had extended negotiations over the price the ferret wanted for the Book of Lore. In the end, the wizard reluctantly gave up his treasured gold pocket watch for the promise of having the book placed in his hands.

Summer days are long days in England, and there are just a few fading rays remaining when the ferret returns.

Rasputin sees the long, skinny, familiar figure slinking past the dozing SnuggleWump. The raven thinks the ferret, long delayed, is at last bringing the Book of Lore that he went to fetch.

Jacko squeezes under the chain-link fence. It is not, however, the Book of Lore that he leaves on the porch. It is the wizard's

KENNETH G. OLD & PATTY OLD WEST

gold pocket watch. He lays it gently down on the front doormat, gives a sharp rat-ta-tat-tat on the door, and disappears like a flash of lightning back up the path towards the croc' pond.

Opening the door, the wizard looks around expectantly. He is puzzled. Rasputin flutters down and explains. "Boss, the ferret left something on the doormat and took off like he was being chased by the devil himself."

"What's this? Why did he leave my pocket watch here? I need to talk to him. Rasputin, my lad, go find him. Tell the creature that all is forgiven, and I need to see him right away."

Rasputin knows the ferret's nocturnal habits and assumes he is down some dark burrow hunting rabbits. He makes a thorough search of the Common and takes a turn out over the bog. There is no sign of the sneaky creature. At last he gives up and returns to the cottage. "Boss, I couldn't spot him anywhere. He must be hiding underground. I think we'll just have to wait until morning to find him. I'll watch for him from the ridge of the roof." The raven keeps his eyes open but isn't expecting to see the ferret before morning light. He is well aware that above him in the ash tree is an owl keeping his vigil also.

Hours pass and the wizard checks his watch, back in its accustomed place. It is close to midnight. Night continues to tick its short hours away, but there is no Jacko. The dawn chorus of birdsong increases. Every bird on the Brook chirps, chatters, or warbles, creating a symphony of harmony as dawn itself breaks. It is going to be a hot day, although distant clouds threaten rain later. The wizard stirs uneasily in his chair by the fireplace. The bunion on his left foot is burning, a sure sign of rain to come.

Rubbing her eyes, a barefoot Griselda Squidge makes her way down the stairs. Cajjer stays under the bed. She has her dressing gown tight about her and hair curlers still massed on her head, looking like the Light Brigade before the charge at Balaclava. Her eyebrows lift almost high enough to meet her curlers when she sees her guest downstairs and fully dressed.

Puttering out into the kitchen, she rakes the coals in the cooking range. There is no sign of glowing embers. Sometimes she's lucky and the fire stays in all night. Not so this time. She sighs and sets about making a fire. Taking paper and kindling, she lights the paper and waits for it to catch fire to the kindling before adding larger pieces of wood. As she waits, she murmurs to herself, "I wonder what we should have for breakfast? You would think, being Cornish, that Griswold would enjoy pickled herrings and canned mackerel with fried leftover porridge, but he wasn't enthusiastic the last time I served that to him."

The wizard stretches, goes out onto the porch, and whistles for Rasputin. He throws a scowl towards the owl in the top of the ash tree and another towards the SnuggleWump. Then, for good measure, he glares up at the teros on the ridge.

Rasputin goes off to search for Jacko once more. He is tired. He hasn't had any good sleep for more than twenty-four hours when he started off for the waterfall from the border control fort with Dr. Tyfuss.

"If it wasn't that my master needs me, I'd begin wondering whether it wasn't time to retire. Ravens get worn out too." It is more difficult for birds to sigh than humans, but he tries. He finds no sign of the ferret and reports this to Griswold. The wizard is not happy.

He wanders into the kitchen to see what Squidgy is cooking up for breakfast. The sight of cold porridge beginning to sizzle in the frying pan helps the wizard make up his mind. He tells his hostess, "I have urgent State business back in Gyminge. I regret I will be unable to stay for breakfast." He sees that the tea is already made. "Just a cup of hot tea will do me fine."

"Would you like a yeast bun with your tea? I can warm one up for you."

"No, not even a yeast bun." The memories of what her yeast buns did to Moley are still fresh in his mind. He is not about to experience some similar fate. He has a final request. "If Jacko turns up, give him a message for me. Tell him that I want to see him right away to discuss employment opportunities. I'm thinking he could fill the new position of Assistant Brook Security Officer, answering directly to you, my dear lady. I'll be back as soon as I get word that the ferret has been located."

Griswold always leaves his hostess with words of praise. "I want you to know that I am deeply grateful for your bountiful hospitality. I'm sorry about the fall you had yesterday while dusting the kitchen cupboards." That's not what actually happened of course, but it's what she told the wizard. "I'll send Rasputin back regularly to get news of your health and, hopefully, your continuing recovery."

The wizard steps out onto the porch and changes himself into a raven. The two ravens head north together. The wizard is in no mood to struggle through the waterfall tunnel. They will fly back direct to the castle. A few quick words as he flies opens up a hole in the curtain. Tuwhit follows them as far as the curtain, but the wizard is past caring. Despite meticulous planning, events have not worked out well. He just wants to get home, but he makes certain the curtain is closed behind them.

Tuwhit turns to go inform the Twith. He drops down beside Jordy who is on patrol. "The wizard and Rasputin just disappeared through the curtain into Gyminge. I haven't seen any sign of Jacko today. It appears that Squidgy suffered some kind of accident. She has a big bump on her head and bruises on both hands. Something also happened to Cajjer. I haven't seen him out on the cottage porch as usual, but I hear him let out little kitten-like whimpers now and again. When he returned yesterday, his face was all swollen. Perhaps he has a toothache. The SnuggleWump's eyes are green, so there shouldn't be any problems from Squidgy or her pets during the weddings."

On the Gyminge side of the curtain, odd thoughts flash through the wizard's mind as he flies. *I wonder where Ambassador Tyfuss is? Presumably the good doctor is still at the farmhouse. Well, the Twith got their side of the bargain even if I failed to receive what was due me.* Although the thoughts are not so odd, his feelings, considering he is the wizard, are unusual. He begins to feel a certain glow of righteous satisfaction. He tells Rasputin, "Men should keep their promises, and I have done so. There are so few examples these days of men behaving honorably."

They fly over the border fort, but they do not notice the ambassador lying flat on his tummy. He sips a glass of cowslip wine as he watches the way woodlouses organize their forces when their housing colony experiences a fire. When they get the fire under control, he finishes off his wine and rolls over onto his back with his arms behind his head. "This is the life! I hope I get at least another week before the wizard returns from the Brook." Just then he spots, low in the sky and heading north, two black birds. He knows immediately who they are. "Oh, no! There are no birds in Gyminge. That means only one thing. The wizard and Rasputin are back! Drat! So much for the good life." He sighs and climbs to his feet.

The Wizard
Has Another
Brilliant Idea

In Raven's Haven on the north wall of Goblin Castle, Rasputin is deep in a sleep of exhaustion. It has been a hard week for the bird, and he is glad to be back home in familiar surroundings.

After his failed trip to the Brook, the wizard is glad to be back in familiar surroundings too. The servants came running the moment he arrived back. He has had a shave and is enjoying playing with his boats in a hot bath. While soaking, he expresses some of the deep thoughts running through his mind. "I have been given a superior brain to use. What new invention can I dream up? How about a Jacuzzi using mice to generate the power? I'll develop a geared-up treadmill that turns a waterwheel." He smirks to himself. "Most great inventions were conceived either after a good bath or a good meal. I'm having both!" Slipping into his black dressing gown and black slippers, he calls to his steward. "You can bring up my lunch now."

Trays loaded with more food than he can possibly eat are soon delivered to his room. The split pea soup is steaming hot. It has to be hot enough to burn his tongue or it gets sent back. Grilled ham and cheese sandwiches, spinach salad, apple juice, blackberry pie, and vanilla ice cream are quickly consumed. Smacking his lips, he thinks, *That excellent meal more than compensates for missing breakfast at Mrs. Squidge's.* As the dishes are cleared away, he gives final instructions, "I am not to be disturbed until I ring the bell? Is that understood?"

It is. The word is passed to all the staff, "The Wizard of Wozzle is not to be disturbed until he rings the bell."

He pulls his easy chair around to face the windows so that he has a view across the lake to the north shore. He savors the view of the large statue of himself that is being erected on the north shore. He smiles with satisfaction. "There was public clamor for it, and public subscription paid for it!"

With his foot he drags over the ottoman to serve as his footstool. On the side table is a first bowl of fresh plucked, dark-red cherries, a plate of orange Jaffa cakes and a tray of Darjeeling tea—freshly made and piping hot. His long, bony fingers pop a cherry into his mouth, and he spits the pip across to the fireplace. The tiny seed misses the copper bowl placed there by the servants in the vain hope that it would catch some of the flying pips.

He kicks off his slippers, looks for a moment or so at his bunion, checks that his other foot is without one, scratches his nose, and reflects on a week that has been less than successful. He grumbles gloomily as Jacko comes to mind. "That wretched creature! He messed up a perfect plan to get hold of the Twith Book of Lore. It was to be a simple exchange of properties, and he snatched it away at the last moment. Now I don't even know if the Book of Lore still exists. It's possible that he dropped it in the bog and now it is lost forever." He sighs with dismay and disappointment. "It's obvious that Jacko has no idea what happened to it. Otherwise he would never have returned my pocket watch."

He thinks back to five days earlier when he just arrived back from the Brook with his trophy taken from Twith Mansion. "So much has happened since then and all without benefit." He sits up a little straighter and pulls his shoulders back. "A good leader learns from his failures. It is what a leader with many responsibilities must do. Only I am able to carry so many. Weaker men than myself would crumble. This country is fortunate to have me as its leader."

His attention switches to Dayko's Rime. Squidgy's sister stole the original from the farmhouse when she was disguised as Pansy, a schoolgirl. Before the wizard returned it, he had her make him a copy. He chuckles with delight. "The Twith Logue have no idea that I have a copy of this. Somewhere within it will be clues as to what I should do next."

One of its lines now catches his eye. He hadn't paid much attention to it previously.

The Child shall lead on to the prize.

He takes a long breath. Something flashes within. The birth of a volcano begins deep down in the earth's core. The rumblings will not occur until much later. It is like a young salmon in a mountain stream beginning its journey to the depths of the sea. An idea of immense proportions and potential begins its long and twisted journey from the deep reservoirs of his mind.

He almost chokes on a cherry pip that slips from his mouth into his throat. He coughs it up and spits it out. "That prize is probably Gyminge Castle itself. Right? Then I'll counter attack! There is more than one way to fight a war. There was a recipe for a Cornish pasty in the fake Lore." He smirks. "That could be useful. Yet even as a pasty recipe there was something missing. It didn't ring true. My own recipe that the cooks in the castle use would give a more genuine taste."

He stands up and walks across to a shelf in the writing alcove. Picking up the Book of Lore that he stole from the Twith, he grimaces. "This is a testament to trickery and deviousness. But I'm not beaten yet!" He checks what it says about pasties and also about yeast buns. "I'm not sure whether these will serve my purpose, but that is, after all, a mere detail in the larger scheme of things that can be settled later."

He is never more dangerous than when he is down. "This may be the knockout blow I've been looking for! It will be very interesting if it works. I see no reason why it should not." He allows himself a sly grin. His imagination is working overtime, but it is too soon yet for a full-hearted belly laugh.

His eye twitches as he reads. Five days ago when he opened this book, he had hopes of getting rid of his irritating eye twitch. There is no such hope now, but he does have hope for something else. "It will require a little research in the library, but I will soon find what I need. Unfortunately for me, the Twith are immune to what I have in mind."

His eyes narrow as he contemplates his next move. "This time, it will be the Beyonders, not the Twith that will feel the crack of my whip and the full measure of my wrath. My change of focus for attack will catch them completely by surprise. Without the Beyonders, the Twith rebels can never succeed! It is time to target the larger species."

He smirks with satisfaction. "My idea is simple but pure genius! Just over the border of my kingdom is gathered a score of children preparing to invade. One of them is supposed to lead the Twith to the prize." He sneers wickedly. "Oh ho. Is that so? I won't bother to find out which child it is. I'll knock them all out. How? Simple! Inflict them with measles, mumps, and chickenpox to start with. These have long since been overcome in Gyminge but not among the Beyonders. If they survive against those three, how about scarlet fever, athlete's foot, and dengue fever? There's also the common cold, influenza, asthma, shingles, and Legionnaire's disease. To a man of scientific ingenuity like myself, there is a huge choice of genuine diseases available before I even start on all the allergies."

He pulls on his slippers and rises from the chair. "It's time to get to work! I must seize the day! Sluggards win no struggles and doubts cannot overcome difficulties."

In the castle library, the various reference books are soon wide open. Contributors to reference books write on a multitude of subjects and are paid so much per word and extra for illustrations. Many of them are probably overpaid. Some of the publishers' biggest moneymakers are children's diseases. Parents buy whole sets of encyclopedias from door-to-door salesmen just to get the latest information about the diseases their offspring are suffering from or pretending to suffer from. It rarely makes the parents feel better. They would be better off keeping their money and not knowing.

Griswold devours all that the books have to say about his first three diseases. "I'll keep it simple to start with. It shouldn't be difficult for a person of my broad qualifications to develop a virus or two. I might even be able to create medical history by developing one that no one has ever come across before!" He gives himself a mental pat on the back. "Well done, Griswold!

"Happily, each of the three starter diseases is highly infectious. I only have to infect one child and lo! They are all flat on their backs in bed clutching their cuddly toys and crying for mother." He laughs uproariously at the thought and continues reading. "This writer says that a contagious disease like chickenpox is spread by touch. Airborne diseases like measles and mumps are spread by coughing and sneezing. Good!" He makes a few brief notes, closes the encyclopedias but leaves the set of books on the table. His mind is razor sharp, ranging far and wide. "Things are sorting themselves out just fine."

Along with the science of infections, he is already thinking of ingenious ways to serve up his diseases to the children at Gibbins Brook Farm.

He walks briskly over to King Haymun's room. "I have news to share. I'm going to design a new range of functional toys for children. Gyminge children are going to be ahead of the world. Toys should be more than simple playthings. They should be tools for learning."

He gives the king details of a competition he plans to launch. "I want you to collect every Jack-in-the-Box you can find in the castle. It will be your personal assignment, and I trust you will give it your special emphasis. To encourage the children to relinquish their best toys, we will have a competition. The display can be in the great hall. The judging will be at eight o'clock this evening. Arrange your own panel for the judging. The child who wins will get a special prize—a week's holiday from school, a bag of cherries, and a water-ski ride on the back of a cormorant. The parent will receive a week's pay. You can tell them that the Jack-in-the-Box itself will go into the castle museum. Unfortunately, I will only be able to join you for a short while."

The king is relieved to be included once more in the wizard's confidences and sets off happily towards the courtyard to start things moving. He has always been in favor of toys. He has a cupboard full of them and plays with his rubber ducky in the tub.

Griswold is on to his next task. He goes to the laboratory beyond his bedroom. Along one wall is a workbench with various glass measuring cups, rubber tubes, a Bunsen burner, a microscope, and other devices used by chemists and boys making stink bombs. He looks carefully at the shelves of corked bottles holding possible ingredients and nods his head with satisfaction.

He decides, "I'll add in some soot to create darkness. Itching and sneezing powder can be the salt and pepper of the mix." He has soon selected half a dozen bottles to start with. He pulls on his laboratory coat, protects his hands with rubber gloves and settles down to work. All the time he works, his mind is planning ahead. *What is the most effective way to deliver what I'm concocting straight into the farmhouse? Well, I made my way in once before and I can do it again.* He begins to sing as the creative juices start flowing.

He is still there when Dr. Vyruss Tyfuss arrives at the lakeshore, having ridden hard from the border fort in the company of the mail courier. It takes time after he dismounts to be rowed across to the main gate. Sergeant Pimples is apologetic. "I regret the delay, sir. It will most likely be another week before the new drawbridge is ready."

As Vyruss steps out of the boat, he slings the large black overcoat the wizard loaned him over his arm and picks up a shrunken black hat, also on loan. It no longer fits the ambassador and will not fit its owner either. In the other hand he carries a satchel containing a small packet wrapped in a plastic shopping bag and tied with string. He hurries across the courtyard, through the gate into the royal gardens, and up the stairs to the wizard's quarters.

THE AMBASSADOR

Dr. Vyruss Tyfuss has a doctorate in the life of the common or garden woodlouse. He would humbly agree that he is one of the world's leading experts on the habits and culture of the woodlouse. It has been his life's work. He is probably the only person alive able to hold an intelligent conversation with a woodlouse. Lessons from their culture and social habits could, if taken to heart, benefit the whole world. One day he intends to publish the results of his research and dictators will tremble.

The doctor is in the prime of life, probably in his late twenties, just possibly his early thirties. He is clean shaven but looks as though he might be attempting to grow a mustache. His brown hair is combed and parted in the middle. He is neatly dressed in a formal black suit and wears a necktie of modest grey. He is a little plump but, apart from his flatfeet, he has no major ailments.

He is a Twith—there is little doubt of that—a born-and-bred native. Although he is a goblin, something has happened to this man. He no longer looks as though he has lost all hope. There is a sparkle in his eyes and an openness to his face. He appears ready to smile.

Although he knows virtually nothing about medicine, he was court physician to the goblin king, King Haymun, and medical officer for the castle. Haymun relieved him of those duties and promoted him to Colonel Tyfuss, Commander of the Southern Zone. The wizard subsequently appointed him as Ambassador of Gyminge to the Beyond. He no longer regrets his two unexpected promotions that took him away from medicine. He is beginning to enjoy exercising authority.

Vyruss is proud of his tenor voice and sings in his bath with gusto. He has also sung in choirs and especially enjoys performing as a soloist. His most recent accomplishment was conducting the festivities for the arrival of Queen Sheba at the farmhouse last night. At that time, he even included a few on-the-spot compositions of his own.

The ambassador is having difficulty getting in to see the wizard. The nervous steward tells him, "No, sir. I can't let you in. The wizard left instructions that he is not to be disturbed until he rings the bell."

Vyruss insists. "I have very important news from the Beyond that the wizard is waiting for. He will be quite angry if I am not allowed in immediately. I will take complete responsibility for the interruption."

The head steward knocks diffidently at the door to the main room of the wizard's apartments. There is no answer. He knocks again, a little more loudly. *Perhaps he is resting.* Slowly, he turns the handle and peers in. The room is empty. The steward is even more nervous, but behind him the visitor is insistent. The bedroom door is ajar, and the steward tiptoes to it. He is grateful that the bed is undisturbed, and relieved to see a light beyond in the wizard's laboratory.

The strange noise that sounds like a man gargling with tadpoles suggests that the wizard is not sleeping. The steward does not move forward despite the ambassador being so close behind. He takes a deep breath, gulps hard, and shouts, "Excuse me, sir. The ambassador has urgent news." The sound carries across the room and into the laboratory beyond. Quickly he steps away from the door, and Vyruss moves across the bedroom to the far door.

The wizard jerks upright, pulls himself back into the present, and stops singing. He has been peering through his microscope watching all kinds of horrible things happening to the host cells. He turns to see the ambassador."Come here. Take a look, my good man. Viruses themselves may be too small to see through a microscope, but bunches of viruses working together as a gang of invaders can produce very visible reactions. It is a battle to the death. The viruses are clearly struggling hard and fighting well, but they must lose in the end. I produced the host cells by pricking my thumb. Although I was once a Beyonder, in my childhood I was prone to every ailment going around, and I developed immunity to most diseases."

His gives a nasty little laugh. "It won't be so with the children on the Brook. I'll hook every child with at least one of the three prongs of my attack. It will be like Neptune's trident plunging downward again and again! They'll go down like ninepins.

"Come. Let's be seated in the lounge." He takes a last look at the littered battleground under his microscope and reluctantly leaves his laboratory, closing the door behind him. He instructs the steward, "Bring tea for two."

The wizard is all about telling lies. He believes that falsehood is power. When he sent Dr. Tyfuss to the Brook, he changed the direction of his thinking. He instructed the ambassador to only speak truth when dealing with the enemy. Even truth has its place in his master strategy of deceit. But because of that, he decides, *It is not wise to allow the ambassador into my secret thoughts. Knowledge is power. The less shared, the better.*

While riding from the southern border, Vyruss gave much thought about the way to present his news. He wondered whether to keep the Book of Lore as a climax but decided in the end to let the wizard choose. It is safely out of sight in the small satchel Gerald gave him before he left the Brook.

They are seated across a low table on which the silver tea service sparkles and the cups steam with hot tea. The greetings have been brief.

Vyruss does not reach to take a cookie even though he is very hungry and he especially likes Jaffa cakes. He plans to attack the loaded plate shortly. He starts right in. "Sir, I bring important news from Gibbins Brook. Do you wish me to tell you all that happened from the time Rasputin dropped me yesterday morning, or shall I give you the news right away?"

The wizard reflects. *Dr. Tyfuss brought the message that the king agreed to the exchange of the Book of Lore for Queen Sheba to Rasputin at the southern border. I received that, but I haven't actually talked to the good doctor since he left the castle on Tuesday morning to go strike the deal. I am anxious to hear the urgent news, but what I really need is full and complete information about the enemy. Since I'm planning a fresh and secret assault on the farmhouse, I want to hear all the details of the ambassador's experiences there. Every little thing that the doctor has to say may affect what happens. If he shares the urgent news first, he might miss telling me much that could be very important, even critical. I'll let the news come in its right sequence.*

"I will wait for your important news until you are ready to tell it. Start where Rasputin picked you up at the waterfall before dawn yesterday morning. Do not leave out anything. Everything, even what seems a minor detail, may be important. I will judge whether that is so. You have clearly traveled in haste and probably have not taken a meal. Let me first order some sandwiches for you." He rings the bell and tells the steward, "Bring a large plate of assorted sandwiches and a big bowl of cherries. I want the dark-red ones, you know."

It is not long before the ambassador is happily snacking away. While he eats, Griswold ponders his strategy. *I wonder whether the way to deliver the combined measles, mumps and chickenpox attack on the farmhouse is not now sitting before me?* He is also working on a completely fresh idea involving the use of explosives.

The ambassador does not have the remotest idea of what is going through the wizard's mind, which is just as well. He takes one last sip of tea and begins. "I waited by the waterfall until Rasputin gained height to lift me up for the flight to the farmhouse. The wind furled the flag which I carried at an angle. It was still dark, so we were surprised to find other traffic in the sky. As we headed south, we had an unfortunate collision with a rapidly moving object I could not identify. I was dislodged from

Rasputin's grip and found myself dangling from the flagpole although it was not falling. It was somehow supported at the far end and moving erratically through the air. I had little time to explain this to myself except to think the circumstances were somewhat unusual.

"Then a strange flying creature dislodged the flagpole and carried me back the way I had come. I caught just a brief glimpse of it. Oddly, it had wings without feathers. It was clearly not a bat. It appeared to be a pterodactyl, but I couldn't understand how that could be. I thought that pterodactyls were extinct in the Beyond. I also pictured them as much larger. Clearly I was mistaken."

The wizard leans forward curiously but does not seem surprised at news of this strange creature from the past. The ambassador has little idea the wizard is already well acquainted with the titchy teros.

"The creature carrying me was not heading in the direction of the farmhouse and did not seem to be open to suggestions to turn back. I decided that it would be wise for me to leave and make my own way on foot before we went too far, so I jerked free and began falling. An odd-looking duck was flying below me and I landed on that. Although it was not white, it did have a yellow beak and webbed feet so it was certainly a duck. Fortunately, I managed to retain my hold on the flagpole. An owl guided the duck to the farmhouse and we landed in the west garden. By that time, daylight had come."

If the wizard were a boggler, his mind would have boggled trying to make sense of the ambassador's adventures. However, he is a clear thinker—not a boggler—and he merely wonders how it happened. *The doctor appears to be telling the truth, but I don't recall planning it that way. It is strange that Rasputin did not mention the change of plans.*

Vyruss is in a difficult position. He must only tell the truth but recognizes, *I must not betray that I visited the Brook on a previous occasion. The wizard is not aware of that. It is better that he continues to think this was my very first visit.*

VYRUSS CONFIRMS THE WIZARD'S SUSPICIONS

Vyruss pauses in his narrative to have another cup of tea and a few more Jaffa cakes. The wizard waits without comment until the ambassador continues. "The journey was more full of incident than I would have liked, and I was glad to arrive at the farmhouse. I jumped off the duck's back and raised the flag. Your provision to ensure I gained their attention promptly was extremely successful, sir. I called out loudly as you advised, 'Peace! Peace! I come in peace!'

"A man my own size was standing near a large sycamore tree at the edge of the garden. As I walked towards him, he walked towards me. I repeated my greeting. He was friendly and greeted me without animosity. He told me the strange duck was a mallard. Several Twith-size people emerged from a doorway in the center of a log lying on the edge of the field. One of them, wearing a skirt, was the leader of the Twith. His name was Jock. I told him I had an urgent message to deliver. He led me down a long passage through the middle of the log to a large underground room.

"A dozen Little People were gathered around a large table. It was clear that not all of them were Twith. Four among them were girls. One was an old man and one a young boy. The others were varying ages. They decided to have breakfast before they heard what I had to say. While it was being prepared, I was allowed to tidy myself up before presenting myself formally.

"While talking, I was careful to tell them only the truth. I explained that you called me to the castle from my work at the southern border fort and appointed me Ambassador of Gyminge to the Beyond. I told them you instructed me to take a message to King Rufus on the Brook. I let them know that it was only for him and no one else. They acted surprised and concerned that you thought the king was among them. They whispered to each other, but I couldn't overhear what they said.

"I said that if the king actually was present among them, I had credentials to present, and I also had a personal and private letter for him from a woman. I told them that if I could not deliver it, I would have to return to Gyminge with it.

"A big man with red hair wearing pajamas and a bathrobe came out from a corner room. He walked with a limp. It was obvious that he had been eavesdropping. There was a strange stirring in my mind that somewhere in the distant past we might have met. As he sat down at the table, I told him that I needed to be certain that he was indeed the king.

"He did not reply, but the Twith who wears glasses and has a ponytail replied instead. He held up an oversize man's ring with a large ruby in the center of a wide gold filigree band. He explained that only when it is worn by the true King of Gyminge will the ruby glow with an inner light of its own. He said that is the way the Twith have always known from the very beginning who the rightful king is. After he tried it on, he passed it to two others. They each placed it on a finger, but nothing happened. It was then passed to the redheaded man whom they refer to as Cydlo."

The wizard listens attentively. He is completely focused on every word that Vyruss says.

"When Cydlo put the ring on his own finger, I was startled. We watched in awe and complete silence. You could have heard a pin drop. The ring began to glow more and more brightly as though within the ruby itself a bright fire akin to the sun itself was raging. The whole room was quickly bathed in red light. Cydlo said nothing but passed the ring back to Gerald. The light faded as soon as he removed it from his finger. I was satisfied that you had correctly identified Cydlo as King Rufus.

"I presented my credentials as Ambassador of Gyminge to the Beyond that you gave me. He looked at them carefully and told me to proceed.

"I told them about how the queen was removed from her bottle. They listened in complete silence. I explained she gave me a personal letter she wrote for the king and passed it to him. The king was deeply affected when he looked at the envelope. Clearly he recognized the writing. He didn't say a word, just pushed back his chair and returned to his room, closing the door behind him. We could all hear the sound of muffled sobbing coming from within the room.

"While we waited, I answered other questions they asked. They were curious how I got to the farmhouse. I'm not sure they completely followed what happened. They asked me questions about the flag, and I told them what I knew. After a while the king returned and this time he was washed and tidy and fully dressed. His eyes were red, but he was smiling. He reminded me I had another letter for him, and I gave that to him. After he opened and read it, he passed the letter back to me to read out loud as you had suggested.

"The contents of your letter astonished and excited those around the table. The king told me they would have to consider your proposal together. After I explained the manner in which the exchange of the queen for the Book of Lore would take place, I went to rest in one of the bedrooms while they discussed it among themselves. I was exhausted and benefited from the rest.

"They woke me up just before eleven so I wouldn't be late getting to the border by noon as you instructed. I was in a deep sleep and they had to shake me to get me awake. They had been discussing the matter for several hours. There were sixteen of us around the table. Gerald had a thick book in front of him that looked old and well worn. I wondered whether it was the actual Twith Book of Lore. It resembled the book you showed me here in this room before I left.

"The king didn't quibble about anything. He just said that he would accept your proposal on the terms and conditions you set down. He set the time for five that same afternoon, and the location at the edge of the bog where the goblin forces withdrew to Gyminge. He said that place would be known to you. He invited me to question Gerald about the Book of Lore involved in the exchange.

"I satisfied myself that the Book of Lore on the table contained the original, genuine, complete, and unaltered Lore of the Twith Logue and that no trickery was intended. I saw the title of the cure for The Magician's Twitch but didn't try to read what the remedy is. I was assured that no attempt would be made to tamper with the Lore before it was exchanged."

The wizard groans and reflects. "I was so close to getting rid of this twitchy eye. Will I ever overcome the difficulties? It is like climbing a mountain that continually gets higher as the climber gets nearer to the summit."

The ambassador continues his story. "I asked if I might see for myself the location they had chosen for the exchange. I informed them that after I passed my message on to Rasputin, who was waiting for me over the border, I would need to return to the farmhouse to take part in the exchange itself. I was offered a meal, but I wanted to be on my way. The owl carried five of us from the farmhouse to inspect the exchange point. There was a pile of soft molehill dirt, and I stuck my flag hard into it in order to mark the spot. Two of the Twith paced out where the king and I would stand during the exchange. Then they went a farther sixty paces back where the others would stand. They were following your conditions for the exchange word for word. They were not planning any tricks.

"The owl took me to the edge of the bog and then a large, old toad named Buffo carried me on his back to the waterfall. After I gave Rasputin the message, I returned to the farmhouse.

"During the exchange at five o'clock, both you and I saw what happened. Jacko stole the Book of Lore. I have no idea where he came from or how he knew what was going to happen and when. I am certain that the Twith Logue and their friends were not involved. They were taken completely by surprise. All of them were shocked and dismayed."

A Surprise for
the Wizard

The wizard nods. "Yes, I'm aware the Twith had nothing to do with stealing the Book of Lore. Continue with your story."

"Four of the Twith jumped onto the back of the owl and were off like a flash pursuing the ferret. We didn't see them again until after we were back inside the farmhouse.

"No one on the Twith side knew anything about the ferret taking the Book of Lore apart from seeing it happen. They had no idea how he knew about it unless you or Mrs. Squidge told him, so they suspected a trick by you.

"The Twith didn't understand why you released the queen. They assumed, as I did, that you would not let the queen cross over onto the Brook and your action to allow it took everyone completely by surprise. Soon you and Rasputin and the cavalrymen with you all disappeared from sight. We had no idea where you went or what you were doing.

"On our side of the curtain, there was mass confusion. They were not at all disappointed with what occurred. They had earlier accepted the loss of the Book of Lore and did not worry about whether you or Jacko had it. Their assumption was that the ferret stole the Book of Lore on your behalf and that he would hand it over to you. So, although it didn't go as planned, the bargain between you and the king was completed. They believed they had followed your terms for the exchange and there was nothing more left to be done.

"As far as they knew, you could have planned it just the way it happened. The important thing for them was that they had the queen. Everyone clustered around her. Among them was a young woman I was seeing for the first time. She closely resembled the queen and it was, in fact, her daughter. I had no idea she was on the Brook. She was overjoyed at what happened. There was also a Twith man that I had not seen before. He proved to be Ambro, the brother of the tallest of the Twith, Taymar."

The wizard breaks in. "There are more of them than I thought. How many are there altogether? Both Twith and Beyonders."

"As far as I could see, there were eleven Twith, counting the queen. There were also, as far as I can estimate, about twenty Beyonders who can change between Beyonder-size and Twith—size. They do so frequently. There are a few others—five, I think—who seem to fit somewhere between ordinary children and Twith. They always stay small and don't ever become the size of Beyonder children. There is something strange about them. Their clothes are old-fashioned and they don't ever seem to get hungry.

"The eagle carried everybody back to the farmhouse. I went with them. Now that the exchange happened, or failed to happen, I expected that I would soon return to Gyminge.

"Once we were back in the house, the children told the two old folks what happened. They were cautious and puzzled about the ferret. They wondered whether he didn't act on his own behalf rather than for you. If you weren't involved and couldn't recover the Book of Lore from the ferret, you would believe that the Twith betrayed you. You would be sure to react strongly.

"There was a feeling of great joy that the queen had rejoined her family. The king and his daughter were so happy! Suddenly a party was underway in the farmhouse. The children filled themselves up with food and began dancing and jumping around and singing. Some of the children found various instruments, and a makeshift orchestra was organized. Everyone joined in with as much noise as they could make. Only Gerald, the Keeper of the Lore, sat in one corner on his own, just watching. I thought he was sad that the Book of Lore had to be given up.

"The party was well underway when suddenly the four who went off on the owl to search for Jacko came back. Taymar wasted no time and joined in dancing right away. The youngest Twith came hurrying in and handed something to Gerald. I didn't see what it was. The boy leaped into the wildest of the dancing. I had never seen such energy like those children have!

"It was getting late and their leader held up his hands for things to stop. He had some news to share. While they were out with the owl, they managed to recover the Book of Lore!"

The wizard jerks forward. *So this is the news the ambassador has brought! Confound it! Hogs-pudding-and-kidney-beans! The Twith have outwitted me once again. Instead of an equal exchange, they have ended up with both trophies.*

He jumps to his feet, forgets he is only wearing slippers, and kicks the ottoman hard. It hardly moves. "*OWEE!* I've broken my toes!" He hops with wild leaps erratically across the room to the easy chair by the window. Groaning, he sinks into it and cradles his foot. *Forget the Jacuzzi. I'm going to design a footstool filled with marshmallows that is meant for kicking with bare feet.*

He vents his anger, not caring if the ambassador hears. "Am I losing my touch? No matter what I devise, I end up on the losing end of any exchanges with the Twith. Time and time again it turns out this way. I have a whole army of goblins at my disposal, and what happens? They are completely defeated by a tiny rabble of rebels and children. I have the only SnuggleWump in the world and the creature fled from the battlefield in disgrace. I am the greatest magician in the world, but I can't seem to make a single dent in the defenses of the farmhouse. I can change myself into anything I want. They are helpless to change themselves into anything at all. Yet, it makes no difference! They come out on top every time."

He hobbles back to the tea table, throws the bowl of cherries against the main door, and rings the bell furiously. "Bring a bowl of hot water and bandages! What are you waiting for! Hurry!

And clean up the floor. Why are you spreading the mess all over the room with your feet?"

Vyruss is perturbed that his story brought such a violent reaction. He knows it has a happy ending for the wizard, but he wasn't able to get that far. He wonders, *Should I produce the package here and now? No, I better hold off. I'll wait until things settle down.*

The wizard cleans and bandages his damaged foot. Eventually he indicates the ambassador should resume from where he left off.

"Gerald held up for all to see the thing that was slipped to him. It was the same package I had placed at the curtain at five o'clock. I was in no doubt of what it was and neither was anyone else. The celebrations reached an even higher level of noise and activity.

"I noticed that Gerald slipped off downstairs, presumably to return the Book of Lore to its hiding place. He wasn't looking any happier than he was before. Jock and the king and queen also left and followed him. I wondered what was going on, and I didn't have long to wait. Gerald returned and asked me to join them.

"They were sitting around the table that we used when making the exchange arrangements. King Rufus explained to me, very slowly and carefully, that he and the Twith elders believed they made a promise with you for an exchange. Although they would have preferred not to, they felt bound to keep their word. Since I was your representative, they felt that by giving the Book of Lore to me, they would fulfill their promise. I inspected the Book of Lore to make sure it was exactly as it was at five o'clock. I was satisfied that it was. Once more Gerald wrapped and tied it in the plastic bag. As he handed it to me, he said that they would assist me in returning to Gyminge to complete their agreement with you."

The wizard, with a look of amazement and growing excitement on his face, leans forward on the edge of his chair. He mutters quietly to himself, "Incredible! The fools!" He forgets about his sore foot.

Vyruss is enjoying the effect of his surprise. He continues. "I was surprised by their action. They were in great haste, and I was not given any opportunity to say farewell to those upstairs in the farmhouse. I was sorry because they had been very kind and invited me to the weddings that are to take place tomorrow evening."

"The owl was sent for to carry me to the edge of the bog and the toad, the same one as before, carried me across to and through the waterfall and saw me into Gyminge. There was another toad at the top of the waterfall that seemed to be on guard duty. I returned to the southern border fort. I was unsure whether you were on the Brook or at the castle. Major Bubblewick said that you and Rasputin left yesterday afternoon and the watch had not seen you return. When you were spotted returning to the castle early this morning, I came as quickly as I could in company of the mail courier."

Vyruss clears his throat. With a broad grin, he announces, "It gives me great pleasure, sir, to deliver to you, with the compliments of King Rufus of Gibbins Brook Farm, the genuine Twith Book of Lore."

The ambassador reaches into his satchel and removes a package wrapped in a plastic shopping bag and tied with string. With a flourish he hands it to the wizard.

For the first time, the wizard has his hands on the genuine Twith Book of Lore. He heaves a great sigh of relief and satisfaction. "Full marks to you, my faithful ambassador! Thank goodness there is at least one person I can trust."

A Slight Change
of Plans

The ambassador now waits for the wizard's response. He has no idea what is going on in the wizard's mind. Over the years, the leader of Gyminge and Wozzle has developed a multiple track mind. Most of the time, though, it only runs on two tracks.

Currently it's running on six! One track is thinking mottoes. He has lots of them. Mottoes are the jewels of a fertile mind. *A wise man uses few words. To be a winner choose weaker opponents.*

He looks down at the package and slowly begins to untie the knots. He is not one of those who believes that time is money. To cut string saves time, but he is more concerned about being thrifty. He believes that it might be an unknotted piece of string that saves the day if he is searching in vain for a spool of cotton.

More of his mottoes spring to mind. *Waste not, want not. A stitch in time saves nine. For want of a nail the shoe was lost and for want of a shoe the horse was lost and for want of a horse the rider was lost and for want of the rider the battle was lost.*

The second track is thinking that the Twith are fools. He shares his thoughts with Dr. Tyfuss. "Jock and his crew are totally naive. How can they ever hope to win any conflict when they give the victory away to the enemy before they have even looted his possessions? Who but a fool will keep a promise when it is so clear that it will give total advantage to the enemy? Promises must be kept flexible and always used to your own advantage or else disregarded altogether. It shows how dangerous truthfulness is. It leads people into awful mistakes that can, and in this case will, lead to their own destruction."

Another motto comes to mind. *Only fools keep promises.*

KENNETH G. OLD & PATTY OLD WEST

The third track is thinking, *I need to check that Dr. Tyfuss has not been tricked regarding what is in the Book of Lore. I am wiser in the ways of the Beyond than the ambassador is.*

He pulls at a knot with his teeth like a dog worrying his master to go for a walk. The last knot unravels. The shopping bag unfolds and Griswold's eyes light up with delight.

"Ah! At last! This is what I have dreamed of for centuries." The book has an old brown vellum cover and is about the same size as the pseudo-Lore on the shelf that he recently looked at. A long while ago some scribe embossed the title in gold, but it has worn off so much it is hardly legible. He does not need to open the cover and read. He knows from within himself, *At last I'm holding the real Book of Lore.*

There is a leather bookmark in the book with its writing also faded and illegible. He opens the book at the bookmark. The heading on that page has been underlined. *Cure for The Magician's Twitch.* He sighs as a climber might sigh having reached unaided the summit of Mount Everest to find on arrival a table set for breakfast with piping hot fried eggs, sausages, and Darjeeling tea steaming in a bone china cup.

Another track comes into play as his eyes catch the underlined words on the opposite page—*Cure for Measles.* He decides, *I'll study the remedy later, when I'm alone and at leisure.* With growing curiosity, he turns over the page. *Just as I suspected. This list of remedies is in alphabetical order.* The page is headed *Cure for Mumps.* His mental train begins picking up speed. He turns back a few pages. *Yes, there it is.* He momentarily forgets he is not alone and reads out, "*The Cure for Chickenpox.* Glorious!"

Vyruss wonders, *Is the wizard suffering from chicken pox? I haven't noticed him itching, but why else would he think that is glorious?*

Griswold chuckles with amusement. "The Twith have surrendered before the attack is even launched. They have not only given away their advantage, they have lost the means to combat my next attack on them." Another motto flashes into his mind. *Dare to risk! All things work together for good for those who risk the most!*

The fifth track is still in its early formative stages. He thinks best when he talks out loud. He doesn't mind if Vyruss overhears. "I plan to block the tunnel to the Beyond not only at its Gyminge end but also—when the time is right—at the waterfall end. The attacking Twith invaders won't have any children to help because they will all be sick. Once the Twith enter the tunnel, the hole in the curtain will be sealed. I won't even need glass bottles for storing this bunch in the dungeons. While the water seeps in from the sides, they'll be trapped in a tunnel tomb—never to be seen again." He chuckles wickedly.

The sixth track now merges into track four as he wonders, *How can I best use the ambassador in view of these new events and the information he shared?* He said he had been invited to the weddings that are to take place tomorrow evening. That very clearly means that he was fully accepted by the Twith.

For once, the wizard is pleased with the performance of one of his underlings. *He played his part brilliantly and duped the Twith completely. He could rise to be the future Prime Minister of Gyminge in a reshuffle of power. But this is an excellent opportunity for me to have a spy in the enemy camp. I need to send him back there at once to become the ears and eyes of his country once again. It would be very unwise to jeopardize the trust the ambassador has gained by charging him with the delivery of the Measles-Mumps-Chickenpox virus. It will be better for the Twith to think that the good doctor is working on their side and against me, the Wizard of Wozzle. This is the heart of good spying. A double agent.* He laughs with amusement.

Thoughtfully, he sets the book down on a side table and leans forward. "Tell me more about the weddings that are being planned at the farmhouse, Mr. Ambassador."

Vyruss blinks. *I was expecting some congratulatory remarks on my successful errand, not a request for further information.* He

KENNETH G. OLD & PATTY OLD WEST

responds with what he knows. "There are two weddings, sir. One is that of the daughter of King Rufus and Queen Sheba, Elisheba, who will be marrying Taymar. The second wedding is that of his younger brother, Ambro, to Cymbeline who is the niece of the one-footed woodcarver called Stumpy. Both weddings are planned for tomorrow at seven in the evening. The toads on the Brook are busy with choir practice and all the birds and animals on the Brook that are their friends are invited to the reception after the weddings."

The wizard recalls the verse from Dayko's Rime that indicated the exchange of the queen for the Book of Lore.

> *The belt is restored from the fire,*
> *Brides shall process to the byre,*
> *The loss of the Lore gives grief*
> *Though what is that to a life?*

He thinks, *Things within the Rime are rolling into place and growing uncomfortably close. It might just be better if brides did not process to the byre.*

The wizard wants more information. "Where are the weddings going to take place? In the farmhouse?"

"I don't know all the details, but I'm certain they are not going to be in the farmhouse. There was no sign of any decorating being done there. The toads will be lining up along a path to the house next door so surely that is where they will be. That's not the old barn but the old cowshed near the farmhouse."

This is enough for the wizard. He knows that a byre is indeed a cowshed. It means more of Dayko's Rime is coming true. It is time to move. Another motto comes to mind. *In an avalanche, who moves fastest and furthest, survives!* The wizard is a man of fierce determination and lightning decisions.

"Mr. Ambassador, I am taken by surprise at the response of King Rufus. It is good to deal with a man of honor and integrity. You, of course, are another such person. There are so few people who keep their promises these days. There is a terrible modern decay in standards that we older men, who have experienced better times, find deplorable and distressing.

"I feel it is only right and proper that I should respond by returning to the king the incorrect Book of Lore that I happen to have in my possession. I would also like to send some small token of goodwill to the queen by returning to her one or two small ornaments that it is likely she would appreciate.

"I would suggest that you take a rest in my guest apartment, and when you are refreshed, you should have a meal. Then, if you are willing, of course, I would like for you to return to the Beyond. I want your journey back to be quite trouble free. I will make the travel arrangements and probably deliver you to the southern border fort myself.

"Since you have this invitation to the weddings, it would be a pity not to accept it. Remain at the farmhouse until the weddings are over. When you are ready to return, make your way over to the fort. You can journey back to the castle with the mail courier."

SPECS THINKS HARD

Specs has been thinking. He is outside the farmhouse lying on his back in the garden with his hands behind his head. The warm, almost hot, sun begins to slip down in the sky while cumulus clouds play tag in the wind high up above.

For a boy, he probably tends to think a little too much. Thinking is rarely healthy, especially for boys. Girls are better thinkers than boys and that activity is in safer hands when it is left to them. There are fewer crises. Boys tend to take thinking too far. They really should stick to climbing trees or waiting for badgers to come out at dark or collecting moths and butterflies or gluing together model airplanes or bouncing stones on water or most anything at all except thinking.

Specs is not on the meal preparation squad this evening. He is part of the clean-up crew that will move in on the wreckage after all the food on the plates has been polished off. Jared, the youngest grandson from Texas, has such a healthy appetite that his plate is licked clean. If the boys thought they could get away with it, they would recycle it straight back into the clean dishes without a spot of water touching it. But when the boys are on dishwashing duties, gran'ma goes into 'hover' mode not far from the kitchen sink to make sure nothing unacceptable takes place.

Just at present, while he waits for the supper bell to start a stampede, Specs is thinking of unfinished business from five days ago—the day of the circus. He is alone so he talks to himself. It is something that people of high intelligence do a lot. "That day I made an opportunity to visit with Cydlo while pretty nigh everyone else was watching the circus performance. We were downstairs in Twith Mansion looking at our copies of Dayko's Rime. I asked him to look at verse seven and read it out to me.

"Cydlo read it and then read it again paying careful attention to the punctuation.

The armour the flame will withstand.
Salt wind shall blow over the land
For light in the heart of the ring
Shall end the restraint of the king.

"The second time through, he gave no pause between the second and third lines. He looked carefully at the words before him and was surprised. He told me, 'According to Dayko, the salt wind goes with the last two lines. We have been taking that second line as separate from the others and it is not so according to the copies we have.'

"I was pleased that he had reached the same conclusion that I did. We realized that we had copies and that the original Rime that Dayko wrote could have a full stop at the end of each of the first two lines. The first thing to do was to check what Dayko's copy actually said. If our copies were identical to his, there is a message hidden in the Rime for us to find. I was sure that the key to the Return lies in the king's ring. We went to Gerald's office and that was when we heard the noise of smashing glass in the passageway and everything collapsed into chaos.

"Now, since the queen's return, Cydlo has become preoccupied with the forthcoming wedding. There hasn't been time to resume our discussion. The Twith have been allowed only two moons to achieve the Return. The sands in the hourglass are slipping through and cannot be recovered. If there is to be a successful return to Gyminge we must find the true interpretation of what Dayko wrote."

The boy's thoughts run on while the bees buzz among the flowers. He continues his conversation with himself. "What does it mean that...

For light in the heart of the ring
Shall end the restraint of the king.

"What restraint is Dayko referring to? I looked up the word restraint in Gumpa's dictionary. It can mean two things, either of which might apply in Cydlo's case. First it can mean that, because of the light in the heart of the ring, the king will give up holding himself back from a particular action. He will stop restraining himself and go full speed ahead with the battle against the wizard. Or, it could be that during all the centuries when Cydlo was just a woodsman in Blindhouse Wood, he was biding his time and waiting for a sign to move.

"The ring was not available to him until the last few days. Now at last the light in the heart of the ring has proven that he is indeed the King of Gyminge. He is no longer constrained to pretend to be only a woodcutter. The restraint of the king has ended. Those two lines in Dayko's Rime have been fulfilled. With the help of those around him, he should go ahead and reclaim his throne. In this case, the light in the heart of the ring has served its purpose.

"There is, though, a second way to look at that same line. Something stands between the king and his throne. Dayko does not say what it is. It can be the wizard himself, or it can be the magic powers of the wizard, or it can be the defense forces defending Gyminge, or it could be the castle walls, or even the curtain around Gyminge. Whatever it might be, it is restraining, holding back, the action of the king, and preventing him from doing what he wants to do.

"From what is written, it is possible to see the light in the heart of the ring as something active and powerful, something capable of being successful in destroying that mysterious restraint. If, for instance, it is darkness that is restraining the action of the king, then the light in the heart of the ring will blaze forth and destroy that darkness."

What Specs is wondering is, "Does the light in the heart of the ring have some particular quality or power not yet discovered that can destroy even more than darkness? The light within the ring is clearly not ordinary light. It doesn't draw its energy from electric power, or a battery, or some other known source. Its source is somehow linked to tapping into the energies of the King of Gyminge. Not the king's physical energies but some other unknown energies that he possesses. How it might work is not known and may never be known. I can't think of anything like it anywhere else. The Twith do not use magic and yet the light works on their behalf like magic. Strangely, it must somehow be connected to truth. It shines for the rightful king, but not for the pretender who seized the throne. It is almost certain that Dayko was aware of a strange unknown power within the ring and recognized that it alone is strong enough to make the Return possible. He was, after all, well acquainted with the ring and he had the strange gift of seeing into the future.

"The immediate danger facing the Twith before they ever start the Last Battle for the Return in Gyminge is that the wizard will close off access into Gyminge from the cave-tunnel. That would not be difficult for him to do. Once that is blocked, there will be no way for the Twith to get back into their own country.

"Yet at the same time, Dayko himself has no doubt about their Return. He knows it is going to be possible and the key to why and how, in my mind, must lie within this particular line in the Rime. We need to understand what it says so we can use it for the Return.

"I need to share what I've been thinking with Cydlo. After supper I'll ask Bajjer to take my place in the wash-up crew and go talk to the king once more. Perhaps Gumpa will come with me. We have to get to the bottom of the light in the ring and its power before it is too late to matter."

Jordy comes out of Twith Mansion to call Barney in for supper. He sees Specs and says, "Hi. Have you seen Barney?"

Spec responds, "Hi! I did see him earlier. He was playing on the bank. Yes, there he is." He points in the direction of the garage. "Jordy. Will you do me a favor? When the meal in Twith Mansion is over, will you tell Cydlo that I wish to see him on an urgent matter? I may bring Gumpa with me. He could just send Barney over to let us know when is a convenient time."

"Sure. I'll tell him."

"Thanks."

The familiar bell inside the farmhouse rings, and Specs hears the sound of a stampede heading for the dining room.

The Light in the Ring

No time is really a convenient time for the king. He has been reunited with his wife barely more than twenty-four hours. The wedding of their daughter is in the offing. There are many things to talk and ask about. His daughter is anxious to be with her parents, and Taymar is anxious to be with her. Time available is getting limited.

However, Cydlo has been most impressed by Specs and remembers that their last conversation had been interrupted by the wizard at an important point. He sends Barney over after dinner.

Barney shrinks Specs and Gumpa, brings them down, and hangs around himself. He doesn't want to miss anything. "Is it all right if I stay?"

Specs tells him, "Sure. We don't need to see Cydlo alone. If others wish to listen, that's fine. They may have their own wisdom to share after they hear what we have to say."

The Shadow children are out practicing wedding music on the top of the well, but all the Little People gather around the table. The chairs are clustered close together. No one is missing. There is not a word of interruption while the earnest schoolboy speaks.

Specs is brief and to the point as he shares what he has come to believe. "The king possesses some peculiar power that Dayko knows will enable the Return of the Twith to Gyminge. If you don't already know about that power, Sire, then we must discover without delay what it is and how to use it. The key to finding out is the ring. That alone makes the power visible and known. Listen carefully to the words in Dayko's Rime.

Salt wind shall blow over the land
For light in the heart of the ring
Shall end the restraint of the king.

"We only have until August twelfth to complete the Return. Without a doubt, the wizard is going to block the tunnel beyond the waterfall soon. Dr. Tyfuss told us that was what the wizard wanted done at one point but changed his mind. He could easily seal it off any day. What could we do then? We'd be trapped in the Beyond with no way back to Gyminge.

"The first of the three lines from the Rime says salt wind shall blow over the land. That is not happening now. What is the barrier that is stopping the salt wind from blowing over Gyminge? Without a doubt, it is the wizard's curtain. Not even the wind can get through it or penetrate it.

"Dayko was telling us as plainly as he could without spelling it out in tiny one syllable words. He put into the Rime what he dimly saw ahead for us. I believe that the power of the king can, through the light within the ring, cut a hole in the wizard's curtain that allows the salt wind to blow over the land. With a big enough hole in the curtain, there will be no stopping the Twith and their bird friends from returning to Gyminge before the time runs out.

"But we must hurry! There is no time to waste. The clock does not stop while we celebrate. I know, Sire, that you are preoccupied with the wedding of your daughter and the arrival of your wife. But you must make time to wear the ring and find out its secret. You need to learn how to use the light effectively. You have to discover whether the light can be turned into a fire or a sword or some other kind of weapon. Except for the wedding itself, others must take over your duties. No one except you, Sire, can do what is needed to discover the power in or through the ring. You alone, Sire, are the source of its light."

Like the others, Gerald has been listening with complete attention. Without a word being spoken, he rises and goes into his office. He returns just as quietly and passes the ring he fetched, not to the king beside him, but to his other neighbor, Jock. It will pass through the hands of all those present before it reaches the king himself.

As it is passed from one to the other, it is carefully examined as though by looking hard all will become clear. The silence continues. All else has lost significance. Only the ring matters. They have all seen the ring glow when the king puts it on his finger.

It is made to fit a large finger and it is heavy. It is not solid gold but rather a gold filigree band wider in height at the front than at the back. The open spaces of the filigree are filled with rubies artfully cut to shape which gives a harmonized blend of red and gold to the ring. There are almost three dozen rubies thus set. The largest ruby, in the front center of the ring, is pear shaped, larger at the bottom than the top. It is deeper by far than any of the other rubies as though there are hidden depths to it that can only barely be perceived. The skills of both jeweler and goldsmith have combined to produce a thing of rare beauty.

When the ring reaches Specs, he searches for any kind of joint that could permit one or more of the jewels to be twisted or swiveled. There isn't one. Each of the rubies is strongly set. There is nothing loose and there are no tiny hidden mechanisms within the ring. He passes it on to Gumpa who takes less time to examine it and pass it on to Queen Sheba. It has almost completed its journey.

What Specs said about the wizard closing the tunnel has been bothering Gumpa. He asks a question. "I would like to ask Jock whether any watch is being kept on the far end of the tunnel by the toads. Do we know what is happening there?"

Jock responds. "Aye. After one o' our earlier discussions, I warned Buffo o' th' danger o' closure ta th' traditional spawning route. Th' toads dare nay 'ave tha' pathway blocked. They 'ave been makin' regular patrols ta check tha' i' stays open. 'Owe'er, durin' th' negotiations fur th' return o' th' queen, Vyruss told us tha' goblin guards with lamps 'ave been on duty all along th' tunnel. While guards are in th' tunnel, thur is little danger tha' th' tunnel will be closed. I' wuld prevent thur return ta Gyminge. So now thur is a toad constantly on duty a' th' waterfall end o' th' tunnel. 'E is ta make sure tha' th' guards with lights are still in th' tunnel 'n' tha' thur is no activity takin' place a' th' far end. I wuld like ta commend Specs fur wha''e 'as shared with us."

Gumpa continues, "I would also like to commend Specs for what he has shared. It leads me to ask you, Cydlo, when you were king, did Dayko ever discuss the power of the ring with you? Also, did you yourself ever experience any sign of unusual power while wearing the ring? Were you in any way aware of its effect?"

Cydlo answers Gumpa's questions. "Yes to your first question, Gumpa. I did talk about it with Dayko. I was puzzled by the ring. How did it suddenly begin to glow red when I put it on my finger? I had never worn it before I became king. It was known as the King's Royal Ring and it was only ever used or worn by him. Once I was king, it never failed to glow when I wore it. I asked Dayko whether it was the rubies within the ring that had this strange quality or the whole assembled ring as a unity. I wanted to know how it happened.

"Dayko explained that the ring was merely a mirror. I, the king, was the source of the light. The power within the ring was a reflection of the power within the kingship of Gyminge. It is a power only possessed by the rightful king. An usurper could not cause the ring to glow. If the wizard had been able to secure the ring, he might have hoped to make it glow. He might indeed, by some magic of his own contriving, have caused it to glow. However, the ring would not have glowed because of any energy received from the wizard.

"Both the kingship and the ring go back into the mists of early time. The ring affirms the rightful king and him alone. On my other question of 'how does it happen?' Dayko was unaware how the ring and the rightful ruler lock together to affirm each other.

"You asked whether I have ever experienced any unusual power or effect while wearing the ring or have been in any way aware of it. Yes, I have. When Taymar was leaving from the castle for the Beyond, we realized he needed to be able to bring Beyonders down to his size when the need arose. I bathed his hands in the light of the ring. I now remember that as the light strangely focused itself, I did feel power draining from me into him. Later, with Dayko's counsel and help, the other escaping Twith were also equipped with the same power. This gift has been of great value to us.

"That experience caused me to wonder how Dayko ever became aware that there is a hidden power in my kingship. I have to believe that it was something derived from his own knowledge as a seer. But it appears from the Rime that it might be essential to us now. Recognize that this is not a ring I normally wear. I have worn it only rarely. It was used when my father died and during my coronation ceremony. It is here now because I gave it to the High Seer to send to the Beyond when we were attacked. He placed it in the treasure box for Gerald to bring here.

"Let my own response to Specs be gratitude for his counsel. I will keep the ring with me. When I am on my own and the light is not distracting to others, I will try to find how the hidden power of the King of Gyminge can be put to use to ensure our Return. If any of you have any thoughts how I might go about this, please share them with me. Meanwhile, let us be cautious about who we share this information with."

VYRUSS MAKES HIS WAY BACK

In Goblin Castle, Dr. Tyfuss sleeps heavily with a smile on his face. In his dreams, he is back at the farmhouse on the Brook attending the weddings. It is a happy day. He himself is one of the grooms! He will sing an operatic aria to his bride as part of the ceremony. He favors one from the opera *Tosca* by Puccini. Perhaps *Recondita Armonia*. It means Hidden Harmony, which is exactly how he feels.

The wizard has a double and more separated focus. The tracks on which the wizard's thoughts are running have diminished from six to two. They are parallel and must on no account converge, at least until the ambassador has been dropped off at the southern border. Shortly before his ambassador returned from the Brook, the wizard's mood had swung from gloom to glee because of what he read in Dayko's Rime about a Child leading the Return. Now, with the receipt of the original Book of Lore, he is filled with complete confidence.

Track one in his mind has to do with his ambassador. "According to Dr. Tyfuss, the weddings are tomorrow. I have every intention of creating chaos at the farmhouse before then. I would like to have my spy planted back in the mansion well before the fireworks begin to erupt. No blame must fall on the ambassador for what his master is about to do. His story must be completely without guile. I must feed him only the crumbs of truth that can be shared with the beggars around him." Although the other track of thinking is not his mottoes, one pops into his head anyway. *Deception always starts at home.* He smiles to himself.

Track two starts from his laboratory. He is extremely pleased with himself. "Things are going remarkably well. I've added itching powder and sneezing powder to my mix. That will make it more potent. The viruses themselves are chugging along nicely. I had to work on their speed of action. There can't be any delayed effect. One deep breath and ZONK! That's what I'm after." He laughs viciously. "Other viruses may be tortoises; mine are hares! The viruses have learned to live together without killing each other off. They no longer waste time getting acquainted with the enemy. They lunge for the kill before they even arrive at the scene of battle. If only my own men were the same!"

He peers through his microscope. "It is most enjoyable watching a bunch of viruses having a go against desperate defending cells in the same way that yeast reacts to sugar and milk."

Griswold reflects on his brilliance. "It isn't necessary to stimulate natural genius. In fact, it has to be held back. In liquids, a bubble will always rise to the top. I am the bubble and the others, including those in the farmhouse, are thick treacle, stuck to the bottom! That's where they will always be." He hums contentedly to himself as he works.

He eyes the grey-green liquid in the carefully sealed bottle on his desk. "My brilliance has created a unique explosive mixture for the waterfall end of the toad tunnel. For good measure, I added itching powder and sneezing powder to that too. All that it needs for explosion is air. It won't be hard to arrange that. I know exactly where I will place it. When Rasputin recently went through the tunnel, he noticed a shelf in the roof about midway through. When he investigated, he found it was man-made, no doubt about it. He said that the shelf is empty, but, rather strangely, free of dust that might have been expected to accumulate. It can't be seen by travelers coming from the waterfall end. That will serve a very useful purpose."

Still sitting unread on the wizard's book shelf is the real Book of Lore. "Attention to that will have to wait until I get these other urgent matters out of the way. But then...then the whole future will open up into completely new horizons. There are no limits to a man with vision. The sun is shining brightly on me today!" He breaks into song.

While the ambassador sleeps, the wizard leaves his viruses to themselves for a while. "I need to get the items ready I told Dr. Tyfuss I would send with him. It is my response to the stupidity of the enemy in handing over the real Book of Lore. The Twith make a pitiful foe. A man of my ability really deserves stronger opposition. It is like taking water away from a goldfish. It's just too easy."

He prepares two neatly packed little packages and a letter. The first flat, rectangular package, neatly wrapped in brown paper, is the fake Book of Lore that he stole last Saturday from Gerald's office in Twith Mansion. He places the bookmark he just received in the authentic Book of Lore into the pseudo Lore to mark the pasty recipe. "That recipe needs to be checked. As far as I'm concerned, there is a major mistake in it that needs correcting. No self-respecting Cornishman would stoop to eating a pasty made from that recipe." He ties the parcel neatly with string in double knots. As he tightens the last knot, he wonders, *Will the king cut the string or untie the knots?*

The second package is three-dimensional. It is a small, decorated trinket box. On the loose lid is a broad border of decorated mosaic. In the center is a hunting scene with four horsemen spearing a deer in a forest. The wizard places one of the queen's embroidered handkerchiefs into the box to form a cushion. On it he places five rings selected from the queen's jewelry box full of such trophies. They have been in storage since he first occupied the castle.

Each ring has a gold band, although the width of the bands vary. Each is decorated with different jewels and are unique in design. They are rings that the wizard judges the queen will be glad to have. "Perhaps she will share them with the young brides. Should I perhaps place a noxious spell on each one?" Surprisingly, he relents. "No, after all, everyone wishes a wedding to be happy." He chuckles to himself as he places a second embroidered handkerchief over the rings to protect them.

"There's no need for the ambassador to view the contents of the trinket box. I won't wait until he wakes to wrap it. I'll just use brown paper again rather than gift wrap paper. I have some, but I have other plans for that." He folds the paper neatly, paying attention to make sure each fold is straight, and again carefully ties the parcel with double-knotted string. In his untidy scrawl he addresses it to: *Queen Sheba, with compliments.*

Now he turns his attention to the letter. "Keep it brief, Griswold." He does. It is a politely phrased note thanking the king for the genuine Book of Lore and explaining that he is returning the copy that he has found in his possession.

"While I'm about it, I'll do the label that I'll need later. I've decided that I will address the parcel to Gumpa as a surprise gift from one of the children. The old man will surely not open it until the children are all gathered around him. Once the box springs open, the damage will be done and will be irretrievable. I hope the Sellindge village doctor is not away on holiday in Cornwall. Those poor little children will need his attention!" He snickers maliciously.

Griswold opens up his folded copy of Dayko's Rime and lays it face down on the table. On the back are the notes Stormy made about a Farewell Festival. He studies Stormy's handwriting carefully and then practices writing in a similar manner on scrap paper. He reflects. "If I hadn't chosen to become a leader, I could easily have become a master criminal specializing in forging banknotes."

He remembers seeing Pansy hold a pen between her first two fingers and does the same. He writes: *To Gumpa, with love* and then writes it again and again and again. Only when he is completely satisfied that his writing looks exactly like Stormy's does he reach for a label.

The wizard is ready. "Now to get the ambassador on his way." He rings the bell for the head steward. "Bring supper for two in twenty minutes. Advise my guest of the meal time and tell him that we expect to leave within the hour."

The ambassador appears promptly when expected. He is refreshed and hungry. He looks forward first to the opportunity of having a good meal, and then to his return to the farmhouse and his friends there. *I hope I can get back before dark.* The various courses of the meal follow in quick order. Potato and onion soup, trout from the lake and then—for the main course—Yorkshire pudding, roast potatoes, roast meat, cabbage, peas and carrots, and piping hot gravy. He tucks them away as though he hasn't eaten for a month and hardly has room for the sticky toffee pudding with ice-cream. Nevertheless, he eats his full portion and finishes off with, not only a cup of tea, but cheese and Jaffa cakes as well.

The wizard explains, "I am deeply involved with improving education for our children. They are falling behind in the world and I am busy upgrading their schoolbooks. The teachers require additional training and the entire curriculum needs revising. However, I will make time to take you as far as the southern border. Here are the packages I am sending back to the farmhouse with my compliments." He gives the letter to Vyruss to stow with the packages in his satchel. He makes no offer to lend the doctor a second hat. He doubts that the first one he loaned will ever fit him again although he is having it cleaned with hopes that the brim will stretch.

The wizard gives some final instructions. "Remain at the farmhouse as long as you like after the weddings. The longer you stay, the more information you might be able to collect. I will be interested to have your up-to-date news when you return. I trust all goes well with you."

There are still a couple of hours of daylight left in the day. Dr. Tyfuss is quietly confident. *The guard toad at the waterfall I noticed on my return to Gyminge should still be there when I get back through the tunnel. He can go fetch Buffo who will see to getting me to the farmhouse.*

The wizard decides, *A cormorant should be able to manage the job of carrying the ambassador to the border without any problem.* They walk out on the balcony, and within seconds the wizard is once again a cormorant. Vyruss climbs aboard and tucks himself well under the back feathers. The bird lifts into the air, beats his wings hard, and is on his way south to the southern border fort.

THE WIZARD GETS BUSY

The wizard is happy beyond words. It is as though his youth has been renewed. He has made a perfect landing on the lake after leaving Vyruss at the southern border fort. Flying in from the west with the light behind him, he stuck out his webbed feet at right angles to make a glorious rainbow spray. He has another brilliant idea. "When I have more time, I'm going to invent water skis like cormorant's feet to be used by parachutists and hang gliders coming in for a wet landing." Now that he is back to himself and his mouth will curl up, he smiles with delight at his inventiveness.

Griswold is in his laboratory happily drumming little tunes with his fingers on the work top. Through the lens of his high-powered microscope, he watches the shenanigans going on among the first samples of his finished product. "And these are only the first samples! Daniel might have escaped being eaten by lions, but he would never have survived these miniature monsters out for a meal. They are so hungry they would take on an elephant for breakfast and come back for more when they had the bones picked clean. They spend all their free time praying for a larger stomach."

His microscope reveals that the defending cells are reeling and in disarray. "I'm not absolutely sure that all of my various immunities will, even united together, be able to counter my... What shall I call it? The Black Virus is a good name. I better put a mask over my nose and mouth just to be safe. I wonder whether I can create a virus big enough to be seen through a normal bench microscope? After all, I enlarge myself from Twith-size to Beyonder-size. I should be able to enlarge a titchy little virus. What a gift to science that would be!"

A strange, mustard colored concoction simmers in a flask over a low burner flame. When it reaches the right stage of gooeyness, the wizard mixes it with the viruses from under his microscope. Using a glass rod, he stirs them continually until they are blended into one consistent brown color. "I'll allow them time to react with each other and then filter off all spare liquid and leave them to dry."

He gives a wicked little laugh. "I've included so much viral hunger power in this concoction that their invasion into the human body will produce an instant effect. There will be absolutely no incubation period! At the very first sniff, those helping the Twith will drop like flies hit by fly spray.

"Now I need to move on with the design and manufacture of the launch device. What I have in mind is a Jack-in-the-Box. There isn't time to make my own so I've had King Haymun busy rounding up all the Jack-in-the-Boxes in the castle since lunchtime. Time to go see what he's come up with. I may have to make alterations to improve the spring action of the one I choose. I could install a pneumatic ram, and that would revolutionize the toy." He chuckles as he imagines the chaos that could create. "Parents will be afraid to go into their children's bedrooms!"

The children have willingly given up, not only their Jack-in-the-Boxes, but some of their most favorite toys as well in hopes of getting a week off from school.

The wizard makes a preliminary inspection of all the toys lined up on tables in the great hall. He is amazed at the number of children in the castle population. One table is full of teddy bears and on another rest various brand-new toys requiring assembly. A third overflows with dolls of every shape and size. Some look quite well-loved. The wizard is pleased to see how popular the Jack-in-the-Box toy is with modern children in Gyminge. There are more than thirty, in various conditions of wear and use.

The head steward has his eye on the prize for himself and his daughter and places her almost new Jack-in-the-Box in the most strategic position on the table. The box is shamrock green with gold stars all over it and it has a fancy press button release. To his mind, it is obviously the box of choice for its beauty. However, that will not be the standard by which the wizard makes his choice.

The wizard is looking for a box of the right size that appears brand new on the outside. He is not concerned about the innards. He wants a tall Jack-in-the-Box that indicates a powerful spring. It has to have a large compartment for holding his Black Virus, and it must have the right kind of mechanism to secure the lid.

The one he selects is the tallest of all. It is a clown wearing a blue hat, and the main spring itself is a similar blue. The clown's arms are also springs, long and tiny covered in red. The box itself, with alternate red and green sides and a green top, looks brand new. He carefully checks the mechanism for opening and closing. He turns the small handle in the center of one of the sides. As it turns, music begins to play. The wizard recognizes the tune as a nursery rhyme from his childhood days of long ago.

> *All around the mulberry bush*
> *The monkey chased the weasel*
> *The monkey thought 'twas all in fun*
> *Pop goes the weasel!*

Three quarters of the way through the tune, the cover releases. He smiles triumphantly. "This one will do very nicely." The wizard holds up his selection for all to see. There is polite applause, although only half-hearted from the head steward.

The wizard wastes no more time. "I must excuse myself. There is urgent State business to be seen to."

Back in his apartment, he turns on the lights and glances at the clock. Light is fading as evening draws in. Dawn's first light comes early in the morning—between four and five. Then the birds on the Brook begin warbling their dawn chorus. By that time, his little gift for Gumpa must be in place at the farmhouse. "I will use the cormorant disguise to get to the circus field. Then I'll imitate Mac, the foreman at Weasel and Mink Contractors, to deliver my lethal concoction in all its harmless disguise." His laugh is downright venomous.

Walking into the laboratory, he again dons his handkerchief mask. He begins preparing the Jack-in-the-Box to work as his delivery device. "I'll put the Black Virus powder in the clown's hat." He cuts off the top quarter of the hat. Next, he cuts a piece of cardboard the size of the bottom of the hat, leaving tags on each size. He slips that into the hat and pushes it down flat against the bottom. Now he glues the tags to the inside of the hat thus making a firm base. He fills the gaps between the base and the hat with glue, and sets it aside to dry.

He now filters off all liquid from his Black Virus concoction through a cone of fine doubled filter paper. The liquid he seals into a bottle that he labels, *B.V. — Dangerous!* The liquid is probably more powerful than the moist powdery residue. There is a goodly lot of this powder in the filter paper, more than enough for present needs. He spreads the paper flat on a warmed plate of glass to encourage the powder to dry out.

The wizard throws another glance at the clock. He is working against time. The light has faded fast and it is dark outside.

He turns his attention back to the Jack-in-the-Box. Now that the glue has dried, it is time for a trial. Very carefully, the wizard adds table salt to half the depth of the hat. Slowly, so as not to spill the seasoning, he compresses the clown back into his box, tucking in the arms neatly and pushing the head down below the level of the top of the box. With his free hand he pushes the lid down firmly. Slowly he turns the handle on the side of the box until he hears a click that indicates the lid is latched shut.

The wizard rubs his hands together in anticipation. "Now for blastoff! I wish my brother, Glug, was around to see. I rather miss him sometimes." He holds the base firmly with one hand and with the other he slowly turns the handle to make music.

All around the mulberry bush
The monkey chased the weasel
The monkey thought 'twas all in fun
Pop! ....

The lid flies back and the clown springs out with great force as though it is heading through the ceiling. As it is pulled to a shuddering halt by the restraint at its other end, the salt in his hat keeps on going. It scatters all over the work bench and table and down on the floor.

The wizard jumps up and down with glee. "It's a wonderful success! It couldn't have been better." He smiles to himself. "I am really enjoying myself, but I need to be moving on. Time is never neutral. If time is not your friend it is your enemy." He reaches for the mortar and pestle.

NIGHTTIME AT
THE FARMHOUSE

Specs is lying on his bed in the attic. His body is still but his mind is active. All the boys around him are asleep. Earlier in the summer he and Bajjer were alone in the attic. With the arrival of more children, the farmhouse is now bursting at the seams. The girls are below in three of the bedrooms. The brothers Austin and Lucas are in the guest bedroom with Jared, and AJ has the tiny bedroom to himself. Micah and Nick are in the back of the attic on mattresses. There is plenty of room and they are not crowded.

The lights are out, but Specs cannot sleep. He has all of Dayko's Rime memorized and goes through it line by line concentrating on certain words. He murmurs quietly to himself, "The Rime could have been called *The Poem of the King*. It is all about King Rufus. There is one word about gran'ma's chain, and one word about Gerald's belt. But there are nine words that refer to the king. Seven of them are about his equipment. I wonder whether I should wake Bajjer up and talk them over with him?" He restrains himself. "That wouldn't be fair to Bajjer. He sounds as though he is sleeping pretty soundly."

He recites the seven items. "The shield, the sword, the dirk, the crown, the goblet, the armor, and the ring. How many of them do we now possess? All of them! The ring affirmed that Cydlo is the rightful king and Gerald said that the goblet and the anointing oil were used at his coronation to confirm him."

The boy tries to put himself into Dayko's mind. "The old man was seeing far, far, far into an uncertain future that offered only darkness and grief. Dayko knew the battle to save Gyminge was lost. As he was writing his poem, the king was still defending the castle at Fowler's Bridge. That was only for a short while longer.

Peering down the distant lengths of history yet to unfold, Dayko was seeing the land he loved controlled by powers of evil. His world was coming to an end. He could only hold on to the picture he saw emerging within that darkness. That alone offered hope.

"That picture is of the king he knows and loves, to whom he is completely loyal. He sees him returning to the land from an exile that has to last until the time is right. All things must concur to make the Return possible. He doesn't see Cydlo, the woodsman, but the king as he, the High Seer, knows him. The crowned King of Gyminge is powerful and confident, clad in his armor, his sword in his hand, and totally ready for the struggle. He sees the king claiming victory. The Rime itself is a song of triumph.

"The old man sees his monarch in the Beyond from where the Return is to be launched. He knows the location is somewhere with a hollow log, a valiant and victorious dog, reds turning green, an open door, a bog, a byre and brides, and at the crossing point back into Gyminge, a waterfall. From that point it will be straight back to the castle walls to complete the journey's circle. All of those can be identified in or near our present surroundings. All that is left is for the brides to process to the byre—which is Saturday—and for the salt wind to blow over the land.

"Until two and a half weeks ago, Cydlo had never been into the Beyond and the conditions for the Return were as remote as always. The circumstances have changed rapidly and have come together with the king's arrival at the farmhouse. It is as though an avalanche, gathering its force over centuries, is now at the point of releasing itself. Momentum and urgency is mounting as time passes."

The boy hears a mouse scratching, or is it a nestling in the eaves outside? "I wonder whether the king has yet managed to discover the power of the ring? Everything now seems to be waiting on that."

He hears another unexpected noise. This time it is outside. He is at once completely alert. He slips his feet out of bed and feels around in the dark for his slippers. In his groping he finds his bathrobe and pulls that around his shoulders although it is not cold. The attic has no windows, but the boy knows his way well. He has often made his way downstairs in the dark. He feels for the door opening between the two sections of the attic. Beyond is the staircase railing and below is the small landing window looking out on the well. There is a gaining moon. Although he can see the garden, the well, and the sycamore tree, he can't pick out any details.

He continues downstairs. The long room is palely lit by moonlight and an outside light on Uncle Andy's house. There are no more noises, but Specs is intrigued. "It sounded like Dr. Tyfuss. He has a powerful singing voice when he wants to let rip and that's what I thought I heard. Why should he be singing an aria from an opera at this time of night? He is supposed to be back in Gyminge. Can something be seriously wrong?"

Specs is not the only one who heard the noise outside. Barney is down the circular Twith staircase from his bedroom only moments after Specs whispers, "Is anyone there?"

Barney reaches out and quickly grabs the boy's hand to shrink him. "Come on!" He is in a hurry to satisfy his own curiosity. The walls below are luminous, the rooms are permanently well lit by the special Twith paint on the walls and ceiling.

Taymar, on duty outside, brings the unexpected visitor in. Yes, it is indeed the wizard's ambassador, in a very happy mood.

He asks Taymar, "Why are you on guard duty the day of your wedding?"

Taymar replies, "Oh, the weddings have been put off until Saturday."

Vyruss is pleased to hear that the weddings have been deferred for a day. This will give him a day longer on the Brook before he needs to report back. He bows courteously to both the king and the queen and has a warm greeting for Jock.

He wondered to himself as he traveled whether there might be an opportunity to present a song at the wedding. *I'll wait until discussions arising from my arrival have settled down before I raise the matter.* He runs through the various arias he knows and has sung in the past in case someone might happen to ask. *I could possibly compose fresh words to a familiar tune that would allow me to exercise the full range of my voice. There is a good aria from Handel that might adapt nicely.*

Jordy is already preparing a large pot of tea. Barney goes to help him with the cups and mugs. Soon his sister, and probably Elisheba too, will be down and will take over the catering arrangements.

With the tea poured and the chairs around the table occupied once more, the ambassador greets everyone and reports, "The wizard is busy revising the entire education system for the children in Gyminge. It involves everything from teacher training to upgrading the curriculum and schoolbooks. As far as I could tell, the wizard does not appear to have any immediate plans to visit the Brook."

Jock finds that hard to believe. "I doubt 'e gives a plug nickel 'bout children's education. More likely 'e is spendin' time readin' 'n' memorizin' th' Twith Lore."

Dr. Tyfuss opens his satchel and removes the two parcels wrapped in brown paper and the letter. As he hands the letter to the king, he informs him, "This letter was written earlier today by the wizard at Goblin Castle."

The king looks at the clock to make sure that the hands have not passed midnight. They are close. He skims its contents and then reads the letter to the others.

Gyminge Castle.
Thursday July 7ᵗʰ

Dear King Rufus,

I thank you for your recent parcel. I am asking my ambassador to deliver to your wife a token of my appreciation for your cooperation.

I am returning for your records the copy of the Book of Lore that I found in my possession. I draw your attention to the pasty recipe which I feel can be improved.

Yours sincerely,
Griswold Beswetherick-Jacka

Dr. Tyfuss rises from his chair, bows slightly, and hands the king the flatter of the two parcels. He repeats the gesture as he hands the queen the other package, and then sits back down.

The queen looks at her husband, and he nods approval for her to open her package first. Barney hands her a knife so she can cut the string. The wrapping falls away, and she looks at the box a long while without opening it. She studies the picture of the hunting scene trying to remember. *I wonder what trick the wizard is playing now?* She lifts the loose lid and sets it beside the box. Removing the handkerchief, she lets out a gasp of delighted surprise. She bends over and looks closely, but does not remove any of the rings. Smiling broadly, she slides the box in front of her husband.

Just as the ring had earlier passed from one to another around the table, so now in the same direction the box of rings passes around. Last of all, before the box is once more back in front of the queen, it passes before Cymbeline and then Elisheba. The two brides-to-be look long and hard. The rings are superb examples of the jeweler's art.

As the queen looks back at her husband, the joy she feels is reflected on her face. "This is totally unexpected, this generosity from such an evil man. Perhaps he is not quite as bad, not quite as solidly black, as I thought."

The king slides the other parcel towards Gerald. "Perhaps you would like to open this one." He too cuts the string although, had he been on his own, he would have taken time to unravel each knot. He spent all his spare moments today sewing the replacement copy of the Book of Lore that gran'ma printed out for him from her computer. Tomorrow he will bind it in a brown vellum cover. It won't be the same as the original, but at least it will be the Book of Lore. He removes the wrapping from the pseudo Book of Lore and opens it at the familiar bookmark. Skimming through the pasty recipe, he wonders, *What does the wizard think should be changed?*

There is still another unexpected visitor that night. However, no one, not even Crusty, sees him come or go.

A GIFT FOR GUMPA

It is another of those glorious English summer mornings when the world is singing. Across towards Stanford, a late solitary cuckoo gives his unique call. Beyond, high vapor trails from planes leaving Heathrow extend quietly eastwards. The roar of trucks and cars along the motorway is loud in the clear air. The sunlight bounces off high cirrus clouds. The breeze flutters the summer leaves and scatters more sunlight. Just outside the farm gate a chorus of whistles and chirps and warbles hit the stroller's ears. The mallard on the croc' pond exchanges conversation with the moorhens who have just arrived. The whole world, almost, is happy.

Gumpa alone is not sure he is happy. Gran'ma finally decided it was time to break the news. She has just told him, "There will be a wedding rehearsal minus the toad choirs this afternoon at five o'clock. After that there will be a rehearsal dinner, and I'd like for you to prepare some of your special Pakistani dishes for that. I thought we could serve it the way I once saw in a movie. Everyone sits cross-legged around a low table and eats with their fingers from a great pyramid cone of rice pilaf heaped on a bed of cabbage leaves. It's too bad we don't have a snake charmer. That would help create the right atmosphere."

Gumpa gulps and half protests. "That will require careful preparation." Secretly, he is pleased that gran'ma would trust him with such an important task. He heads for the pantry to start collecting what he will need.

Gran'ma stops him. She knows the chaos he creates when he is busy cooking. "You will have to wait a while to get started. I don't want you messing around in the kitchen just yet. Or even in the pantry. You can have it all to yourself right after lunch.

"All the girls will wear saris and the boys and men will wear shalwar kamiz and turbans. Won't that create a pleasant atmosphere? The Shadow children who grew up in Pakistan have used their talents to come up with suitable clothing. They have been working on that when free from their other duties. I swore them all to secrecy. There are certain occasions, such as weddings, birthdays, and Christmas, when—in my opinion—secrets between couples are acceptable. Don't you agree?"

Gumpa has mixed feelings about that. What concerns him now, however, is that he will be responsible for the entire meal, and he isn't even allowed into the pantry to go through what is available. He wonders, *Where will I get peppers and chilies? I'm definitely going to need some help. After breakfast I'll go down to Twith Mansion and ask the Shadow children to help me. They will surely have some good ideas.*

Stormy has made it her responsibility to bring in the mail. Ever since her arrival at the end of May, she has been the mail girl and counts it one of her favorite jobs. She has to go out to get the mail from the free-standing green mailbox. With four families all getting mail in the same box, it all has to be sorted. And now with all the children here for the summer, there are many more letters to sort through.

All the letters to go out lie overnight on the hall table. Before breakfast Stormy gathers all the outgoing mail and puts it in a plastic shopping bag. She hangs that over the knob on top of the mailbox for the postman to collect. His name, perhaps it is a nickname, is Hermes. He used to come by bicycle, but now he has a little red van. He is plump and has a walrus mustache. He is double-jointed and can also twitch both ears and wiggle his eyebrows. These gifts have brought him a certain notoriety among the customers along his route but not promotion in his job. If there is only a little mail, he puts it in through the brass flap in the front of the mailbox. These days, he puts an elastic band around it, opens the door at the back of the mailbox, and dumps it all in. There is never a day, except Sunday of course, when there is not mail for Gibbins Brook Farm.

Stormy likes to wait right at the kitchen window after breakfast for Hermes to arrive so that she can run out and welcome him. It allows her to sort the mail for the various households before someone else does.

This morning Hermes is early and she is still having breakfast with the others. The custom in the farmhouse is that everyone remains at the table until the very last person has finished polishing off his plate with the crust of his bread. All the children know that it is always the oldest grandson from Texas! As soon as AJ looks up, wipes his lips, and returns his napkin to his napkin ring, the flood of pent up energy to be about other things is released.

As they wait, Gumpa demonstrates once again that the empty shell of a boiled egg needs to be squashed completely flat in order to be safe from goblins. Stormy hears the little van and is anxious to run get the mail. She looks pleadingly at Gumpa. "May I please be excused, Gumpa?"

Gumpa knows that mail from home is a very important facet of the children's lives. He also knows how important it is to Stormy to be the one who sorts it. "Yes, of course. I'll take your plate out."

With a grateful look, she flings a "Thank you," as she pushes back her chair and darts through the door.

Through the window he watches her sorting the mail at the mailbox. The mail for Uncle Andy and his family will remain in the box and the farmhouse mail alone will come back with her. He sees her looking carefully at something else. It looks like a little parcel has also come, and she pops that into the bag.

Stormy is in with the mail and the children wait around the dining table to see if there is a letter from home for them today. One by one the letters are distributed. As usual, gran'ma and Gumpa receive the most.

Finally, after everything else has been dispensed, Stormy produces, with the air of a magician producing a bulldog out of a hat, a glittering gift package with no outer wrapping. With great gusto she announces, "For Gumpa! It doesn't say who it's from. Oddly, it looks a lot like my handwriting but I don't know why. I didn't put it in the mailbox."

It is indeed a gift package. It is a gold-paper wrapped cube about three or possibly four inches on each side. On one side there is a small bump that alone spoils the perfect cube shape. The wrapping paper is neatly creased, too neatly for a child to have done it, so there must have been a parent's help. It is tied with red and white party string. The knots are single knots.

Additionally, a silver ribbon is tied in a neat bow and goes horizontally around the perimeter for decoration. On the top is a hand-written stick-on label: To Gumpa with love. With a sly little grin, Stormy passes the mysterious gift, not to Gumpa, but away from him. She says, "Pass this to Gumpa, will you?"

While Gumpa waits for the little package to make its long journey around the table, he wonders, *Who in the village could have asked Hermes to deliver this with the regular mail? It doesn't appear, from the glimpses I can see, to have stamps or to be properly addressed. Hermes does have children, but they are little terrors bound to become either vagabonds or deadbeats when they are older. It is unlikely to be one of them.* He sees that the children are all examining the writing and whispering speculations to themselves as they pass the package on. He thinks, *One of them may well have secretly placed it in the mailbox and just be pretending to know nothing about it.*

The package finally completes its circuit and is placed into Gumpa's hands. Gumpa is a student of handwriting, and he can tell at once that the cursive handwriting is a girl's. English and American handwriting are very different, so he is fairly certain, too, that it belongs to an English girl. A girl or a woman's handwriting is more round and flowing than a boy's or a man's. It is not difficult to hazard an age either. He thinks, *I would venture this particular writer is somewhere between nine and twelve. My guess is Ginger or Vickie. Vickie may have had the best opportunity to plant it unseen into the mailbox.*

All the children are waiting anxiously for him to open the package. Gran'ma, who is quite accustomed to Gumpa and his treatment of gifts, is half expecting what actually happens. Some of his surprise gifts and parcels have remained unopened for weeks.

"Well, it's time to be getting on with our day and there's lots to do. We'll leave opening this until we have more time."

There is a collective groan of disappointment. Chairs slide back. There is a general rising from the table. Gumpa places the gift parcel on the sideboard and goes to the red room to look for his Indian curry recipe book.

The children take their own letters and go off to find places to read them and, perhaps, shed a few tears.

Arrangements for the Wedding

Since Gumpa is not allowed in the kitchen until after lunch, he goes into the long room and sits in his usual chair near the fireplace. He puts both feet on the back of Lupus, the wolf-dog. On the arm of the chair are Cydlo, Jock, and Gerald. Cydlo is in a similar situation. His wife and daughter have abandoned him as they make last minute preparations for the upcoming wedding.

Gumpa asks Cydlo, "Who will conduct the wedding ceremony?"

The king replies, "That would be Gerald. It will be his first official duty as the High Seer of Gyminge. I had thought I would be doing it, but gran'ma insists that I will escort the bride. I thought that might be a problem now that I have a wife to consider, but she said that I shall still escort my daughter, and I am proud to do so."

Jock is well acquainted with the customs of a Scottish Twith wedding and is curious to know whether these weddings will be the same. "Wha' are th' customs o' yur traditional Twith weddin's?"

"Our wedding service is simple. It is based on openness and truth. Before their wedding day, the couple will share any secrets they have in private. They are eager to share everything because they know it is important to not have any secrets from each other. Successful marriage is based on trust. Secrets destroy trust.

"The couple answers basic marriage questions: 'Are they free to marry?' 'Do they wish to marry?' and so on.

"The main focus of the entire ceremony is the breaking of the eggs. It illustrates the merging of two lives into one as they are united in marriage.

"Following that is the joining of hands creating a circle that represents the continuity of their love.

"Sometimes the couple decides to exchange rings.

"The High Seer announces that the two are now husband and wife and the couple kisses as a seal to their union."

Jock nods. "Aye, tha' is vury similar ta our wedding' ceremonies 'cept fur th' breakin' o' th' eggs. I'll be interested ta observe tha' part' o' th' ceremony."

Cydlo is concerned. "Gran'ma has overlooked one very important part of the ceremony. It's understandable as she isn't familiar with our customs. The father of the groom has a big part to play. After the breaking of the eggs, he is responsible for preserving them in a glass goblet, covering them with wax. However, we don't have the father of the grooms." He turns to Gumpa, "Would you be willing to take on that responsibility? I'll have to ask Taymar and Ambro, of course."

"Yes, I'd be happy and honored to do that. But only if the boys concur."

The four men break off their discussions for the time being. Cydlo says, "So far, everything seems to be under control." He chuckles. "That's gran'ma's control, of course."

Gumpa stands up. "I'll take Lupus out for some exercise. I need some myself." In normal quieter times, Gumpa and gran'ma take a daily walk down to the pond. Since his arrival, Lupus has deemed they need someone to defend them against predators and robbers and insists on accompanying them. Today gran'ma is too busy with other matters.

Uncle Andy's son-in-laws are busy mowing all the surrounding lawns, including the field at the back.

Gumpa smiles to himself. *Now that Andy can see the Twith, he can give his son-in-laws a commentary of what is happening during the wedding. They are not likely to be able to see the Little People for themselves.*

As Gumpa heads down the path, he sees Andy and Jordy busy working together supervising the transformation of the former cowshed into a mini-cathedral. He steps inside to take a look.

Uncle Andy has placed a wooden ramp from the lawn into the sun porch and another one from the floor to the hearth. Austin and another grandson from Washington, Micah, have neatly covered them with red carpet.

Gumpa, planning ahead in case of rain asked Mike's mother, Sarah, to make a portable canopy to protect the procession of the brides against the weather. The canopy will be carried on four pairs of toothpick poles by two girls in the front and six boys. Sarah used some pretty yellow and white waterproof material. She decorated it with some hanging fringe left over from an upholstery repair. She also made two smaller canopies—one for each end of the red carpet.

The area where the Twith-size congregation will sit is crowded with forty tiny chairs. Stumpy has been hard at work the last two weeks making them. Along the wall opposite the windows are the Beyonder chairs for Uncle Andy and his family. The viewing platforms outside the large picture window are ready for the birds, the rabbits, and the badgers. Blackie and Bandy, although honored to have been invited to sit inside, will watch from outside the window with their friends.

Gumpa strolls on down to the croc' pond where he hears Squidgy across the way. She no longer has any visitors and, in spite of her pain, is singing while weeding and poking around in her garden. His eyes skim the surface of the bog searching for signs of a marsh orchid. This rare plant is an endangered species but they do grow on this particular bog. He walks on down the road a bit and sees one out in the center of the bog. Satisfied, he turns to go back to the farmhouse.

Gumpa is anxious to have lunch over with so he can start preparations for the Indian food gran'ma wants for dinner. While he waits, he tells gran'ma of the morning's discussion. "I have been asked to be the groom's father. I am told that I have a big part to play in the ceremony."

Gran'ma is already aware of the four different parts of the wedding ceremony itself, but the fact that Gumpa will have a part is news to her. "What part do you play?"

Gumpa explains about the sealing of the eggs and gran'ma nearly panics. "I'll have to find out what all is needed for that. Whatever it is, I hope we have it on hand."

THE REHEARSAL

Only those actually involved in the ceremony itself are present for the rehearsal. All the others are invited to the dinner afterwards however. Security is more relaxed with the news that the wizard is involved in updating schoolbooks. Nevertheless, Lupus prowls around the house on the alert. Crusty and Tuwhit both have charge of the airspace for the time of the rehearsal. Two little sparrows, Sparky and her brother, watch Squidgy's cottage, but all is quiet there.

The two couples have agreed that Taymar and Elisheba will marry first, and Ambro and Cymbeline will follow. There will be no honeymoons until they are safely back in Gyminge. Until then, the couples will stay right at Gibbins Brook Farm.

To save time, gran'ma decides to not rehearse the processional from Twith Mansion to the byre. Tomorrow, her granddaughter, Rachael, will be responsible for the departures from Twith Mansion at regular intervals. For now, all the participants are gathered near the door of Max and Julie's sun porch. Gran'ma stands with them to send them forward at the appropriate intervals.

The Shadow children choir, the soloists, and their conductor will already be seated before the processional begins. Gran'ma instructs them to go sit in the chairs on the far side of the hearth. Vyruss is the conductor and is disappointed the rehearsal is not including any of the singing.

Gumpa will also be in place before the ceremony starts, and this is where he would be sent forward. However, he has pleaded to be excused so he can tend to the finalizing of the dinner. Gran'ma has agreed. He has been in the kitchen all afternoon and smells of curry spices anyway.

The last to be seated before the actual processional begins is Queen Sheba. Jordy escorts her to her seat.

Now it is time for Gerald to be sent down the aisle. When he is positioned, Ambro goes forward followed by his best man, Barney. Now gran'ma sends Nick, her grandson from Idaho, on his way. He is Ambro's official ring bearer. All three go sit in the chairs at the side of the hearth. Next, it is Taymar's turn followed by Jock and Lucas. They stand to Gerald's left.

Next will be the flower girl. Titch, the youngest granddaughter, holds an empty basket. Gran'ma tells her, "Even though you don't have any flower petals in your basket, you can pretend to toss the petals to each side as you go down the aisle. Tomorrow it will be filled with rose petals to scatter as you walk." Gran'ma watches until the girl is halfway down and then starts Cymbeline's maid of honor, Ginger, down the aisle. Titch takes a seat in the front row, and Ginger goes up the ramp to sit at the end of the row of chairs where Ambro is.

Next, a beaming Stumpy gallantly takes his niece forward. He has fashioned himself a new wooden leg of walnut for the occasion. It is highly polished. They ascend the platform where they take their seats. Cymbeline sits next to Ambro. The next down the aisle is Elisheba's maid of honor, Stormy, who goes to stand at Gerald's far right. As Cydlo steps forward to escort Elisheba, gran'ma calls to everyone to rise.

Cydlo has no idea what his wife is going to come up with for the actual wedding tomorrow, but he has an opportunity tonight to show what he would have chosen had he been allowed to have his own way. He is wearing his best clothes from the cottage in Blindhouse Wood that Elisheba brought with her. He is bare headed. Around his waist is his heavy leather belt. Normally he would wear his scabbard on the left-hand side so that his right hand can swing across and draw the sword in one quick movement.

However, Elisheba rests on her father's left arm, so for the wedding, the scabbard and the dirk are reversed in position. As he brings her onto the wedding platform, he glances down at the happy girl beside him. He thinks, *She reminds me so much of her mother many years ago. How alike they are! She is the very image of my own bride.*

Gran'ma makes her way down the outside edge of the rows of chairs to slide in next to Titch.

With everyone and everything positioned for the start, Gerald now asks Taymar and Elisheba to make their separate ways to the two high-backed chairs for the Sharing of Secrets. They won't actually share tonight, so they return almost immediately.

Cymbeline and Ambro watch carefully. Their turn will come soon, and they can benefit from what they see Taymar and Elisheba do.

Gerald runs through the various questions he will ask of each couple.

Cydlo places his daughter's hand in Taymar's and quietly withdraws to sit beside his wife.

The rehearsal continues until Gerald is ready to declare the first couple married. Although he pronounces them husband and wife, it won't be official until they kiss at the actual wedding ceremony tomorrow. Then, without pause or delay, the exchange of positions takes place as Cymbeline and Ambro occupy the central space before Gerald. Stumpy comes forward and stands proudly beside his niece. Steadily the rehearsal moves forward.

Mentally, Vyruss is composing a few additional verses for himself and Katie, one of the sisters from Michigan. He scribbles notes on the edge of a newspaper lying nearby that is meant to be used to start a fire. His thoughts turn to something else. *I'm getting increasingly hungry! I wonder how much longer before we move on to the dinner. I've never had Indian curry before.*

At last the rehearsal is over. There have been no major snags. Everyone troops over to enjoy Gumpa's special curry. The smells transport the Three Twithketeers back to their time in Pakistan. Taymar exclaims, "Oh, yes, Gumpa. You got the taste just right!" All the children and Little People alike join in agreement. Gran'ma smiles with satisfaction and Gumpa just grins as he helps himself to another serving.

A Summer's Day

There are poor summer days and there are good summer days. Occasionally—perhaps once in a decade—there comes a day that is beyond improvement. Those are days to be remembered forever. Grandparents, thinking of their distant past, choose—of all their childhood summers to remember—a day like this day. This is the kind of day when children hope that time will stop forever—at least until dinner time.

It is warm and promises warmer but not so hot as to be stifling. The southwest breeze is friendly and will likely be around throughout the long hours of the midsummer day. The leaves on the trees are waltzing. The high cirrus clouds suggest a beautiful sunset later. The weather girls on TV are all smiles, as though the credit for what is happening depends on them, and they deserve a bonus for having arranged it.

It is a day when even ferrets feel friendly towards rabbits and sympathetic towards any bereavement they have caused some mothers and fathers. It is a day when road crews strip to their waists and sing as they shovel and toss dirt out of trenches. They pity those who have to sit at desks in stuffy offices. It is a day when mothers forgive their children for stuffing their dirty clothes under the bed and wives forgive their husbands for being absent when the children need a firm hand and sound discipline. It is a day when children are off to the beaches and the rock pools, and feel that the fun they've had will be worth the consequences of arriving home with wet and muddy clothes.

It is a day when birds everywhere sing at the top of their voices, toads burp and their choirs gargle in readiness for the evening festivities. Housewives do their washing with never a look at the sky, and Griselda Squidge thinks only sad instead of viciously unkind thoughts about her runaway husband and the sweetshop girl. It is a day when old Mr. Rutherford thinks Sellindge is likely to win the competition for the prettiest village in Kent, and the Reverend Jeremiah Toppling of St Mary's Anglican church is encouraged about the state of the church tower.

It is a day when even Griswold, the Wizard of Wozzle, is singing although the music is not of high quality. His mouth is involved in consuming perfectly ripened, sweet, dark-red cherries which interrupt the melody he tries to sing. He is at home in the large hall of his suite in the north wing of Goblin Castle.

He rubs his hands together with pleasure. "Things are going well, very well indeed." He spits a cherry pip towards the back of the fireplace. Surprisingly, it bounces into the copper bowl. Griswold hears it ding and decides, *It is a good day for target practice. I have plenty more cherries in that crystal bowl.* He reloads.

His mind turns to unfinished business. "I need to work out what to do about the tunnel. It is the one weak link in defending my kingdom. The impenetrable curtain surrounding both Wozzle and Gyminge has been immensely successful. Except for one thing. It doesn't block the toad tunnel into Gyminge. Long, long centuries of previous use by migrating mother toads keeps the curtain open at that point. Even though I concocted stronger formulas for the curtain, they had no effect. The toads just keep on coming and going year after year. Even worse, the Twith discovered the way into Gyminge through the waterfall and used the tunnel to rescue gran'ma. Somehow, I have to solve the problem of closing the tunnel even if it means upsetting the toads.

"Dayko's Rime allows the enemy at Gibbins Brook Farm only a matter of weeks for their attempt to wrest the kingdom from my hands. I'm going to block the toad tunnel to make sure no one gets through until well after the time available for the Return has elapsed. Then it will no longer matter if I reopen it for the toads.

"I have already accumulated all the stones necessary to build a thick wall to block the Gyminge end of the tunnel. To prevent the toads or the Twith enemy from working inside the tunnel to remove the stones, I'll put pipes through the wall. That will not be difficult. Anyone in the tunnel can be sprayed with itching, coughing, and sneezing powders as well as other noxious substances including gases and offensive smells. The manufacturing of these helpful substances is well under way and they merely need packing and a method of delivery.

"I also plan on blocking the other end of the tunnel. Because a curtain doesn't work to block it, it will require using explosives. I've never had to use explosives in the past, so I've read my reference books carefully. The explosives themselves are not difficult, but they need some kind of a trigger to set them off."

Three more cherry pips have landed in the copper bowl. The wizard is a bit disgruntled, however. "I've been waiting patiently for news from my ambassador. My gift to Gumpa should have been opened yesterday, and I expected Dr. Tyfuss to flee back to the southern border fort. He should bring news of the raging epidemic in the enemy camp. As soon as he is safely back, I can proceed with my plans for blocking off the tunnel. I still need to plant the explosives inside the tunnel. But then I shall move forward and order the blockage of the tunnel at the Gyminge end. I can just sit back and relax within my fortress as the remaining possible days for an attack on my territory ebb away.

"I wonder whether I should invite my next-door neighbor, King Haymun, to tea? This is perhaps a good opportunity to share with the neglected monarch the events that have recently been preoccupying my time. Until now, they have necessitated the utmost secrecy. I also need to catch up with the king's activities on revising and bringing up to date the schooling for the children of Gyminge. I have one or two ideas of my own that I want to share with him. Homework needs to be doubled! After tea is over and the king returns to his own apartments, I'll settle down to the read I've been promising myself of the true Twith Lore. It is time I got rid of The Magician's Twitch."

He rings the bell for the head steward. "Bring tea for two at once, and tell King Haymun he is invited for tea." Again the cherry pip dings into the copper bowl. "Well done, Griswold! Tra-la-la-la-la!"

FINAL PREPARATIONS FOR THE WEDDING

On the Brook, a wide variety of activities is going on in Twith Mansion and in the byre and in the farmhouse.

Titch, the youngest granddaughter, and Jenn, the granddaughter from Idaho, are excited to have been chosen to work on the flower arrangements for the wedding. They have been over in the byre with Vickie since right after breakfast. Vickie's aunt Julie has a lovely garden profuse with blossoms of every kind. Julie is giving the girls helpful guidance on decorating when needed. The room is a profusion of colorful flowers, ferns, variegated leaves, and dangling vines. Several bunches of purple grapes from Gumpa's porch have been snipped and repositioned as though their natural home is around the picture frames. Jared and Micah have been warned they must wait until the wedding is over before sampling the grapes.

The roses are particularly beautiful this summer. Wherever there is a ledge or a shelf in the byre, there is a vase filled with roses. Vickie's mother, Sarah, made the two bouquets for the brides. They were shrunk and passed to Barney to remove any thorns. Gumpa sighed as he saw his special red American Beauty and yellow Gold Medal roses go the way of the others. *Well,* he thinks, *it's all for a good cause.* The flower party still has to work on the boutonnieres, corsages, the nosegays, and Cymbeline's headpiece.

The meals for the day are laid out buffet style in both Twith Mansion and in the farmhouse kitchen. Surprisingly there is nothing left over from the huge rehearsal dinner last night. As hunger strikes, and for one or two of the boys it seems to be striking almost continuously, people help themselves to food and drink and then resume their tasks.

After lunch, to keep Taymar and Ambro out of the way, they have been instructed to help rearrange the upper apartment that until now has been Stumpy and Barney's home. No longer! The two young couples are going to share this apartment until the Return to Gyminge. Stumpy's workshop will be moved downstairs to the mansion for good to make space for a living and dining room for the two couples. Cymbeline will retain her old room, but Stumpy and Barney's room will become the first home of Taymar and Elisheba.

The Shadow girls—Ellie, Ruthie, and Margaret—provide the female touch to the rearrangements upstairs. Furniture is moved around. Vickie carries two double beds and a dining table with four chairs from her doll houses up to the only bedroom in the farmhouse with windows facing both south and west. Next to the wardrobe is the entrance into Stumpy's workshop. She picks up the four single beds that Taymar and Ambro pushed out of the way. She will put those in her doll houses instead. Ruthie and Ellie direct the brothers as they tug and push the new furniture into position. Margaret makes sure that everything is neat and tidy, and the boys are sent off to bring up any of their clothes that they won't need for the wedding. Then it will be time to get ready for the ceremony.

Barney's armory of catapults, his exceptional collection of the most amazing junk and clutter, Stumpy's stock of wood pieces, his unfinished carvings, and his stock of completed carvings have all been packed up. Specs and Bajjer carry these treasures along with the clothes, around to the outside entrance of Twith Mansion. Some minor shuffling takes place there. Jock and Jordy will remain in their room, but Gerald will now share his room with Vyruss so Stumpy and Barney can have the second guest room.

Gran'ma turns her husband out of their room for the day. She tells him, "I need the bedroom for the brides and their attendants. I'll lay out your clothes in AJ's room. Perhaps you should practice boiling two eggs without eggshells so you won't have any problems during the ceremony."

Gumpa grins wryly. He had thought the same thing.

The door is closed and the girls are determined that neither Taymar nor Ambro is going to have as much as a whiff of his bride until they meet in front of Gerald shortly after seven this evening. Cymbeline shall not be seen even by her uncle or her brother until it is time. Each girl sits quietly while having her hair done at the same time as her fingernails and toenails.

Rachael and Jenn are the hairstylists. The three Shadow girls and a number of the Beyonder girls have displayed a variety of hairstyles the last week as Rachael and Jenn practiced their skills. They produced some very interesting hair arrangements.

Elisheba's hairstyle for the wedding stimulated much discussion, but she did not want to change her hairstyle until the wedding day in order to keep it a big surprise.

Taymar is blissfully unaware of this. He loves Elisheba's hair just as it is; loves to touch and stroke its looseness with his fingers and has no idea that any change is planned.

On the other hand, Cymbeline's hair has been piled high in repeated tumbles of gathered twists and curls. She has been surprised by how different she can look—almost like a different person. It even made her feel different, and she liked the changes the girls made to her hair.

The wedding dresses are given one last pressing. Stormy and Ginger hurry off to get dressed. Vickie and Jenn deliver the corsages and nosegays. After that, they will take the boutonnieres down to the mansion.

Suddenly Jared, dressed in his best clothes and wearing a grin as wide as his face, starts ringing a hand bell beginning in the farmhouse attic. The boy yells at the top of his voice. "Half an hour to seven o'clock! Half an hour to seven o'clock!"

He moves down the stairs to the bedroom level, stirring up chaos. He has been looking forward to this particular moment for days. A panic of movement starts all around him. Boys and girls suddenly skid in all directions.

Gran'ma alone seems to be ready, dressed in her dark blue dress with the white lace collar that she wore when she married Gumpa. She slips her feet into the dark blue shoes with large silver buckles.

Gumpa, as he scurries upstairs to get dressed, encounters the bell ringer on his way down to the main floor. He remembers, *Oh! I forgot to get the raisins out for the Raisin-Fest.* He quickly reverses direction, narrowly avoiding a collision.

"Half an hour to seven o'clock!" Jared stands by the fireplace hearth and the bell ringing reaches up to Cymbeline's empty apartments and down into every corner of Twith Mansion. He darts into the kitchen for a quick last snack, and meets Nick and Micah who got there before him. They are just leaving—their mouths are crammed full—and they are unable to speak.

Outside the window, near the well, the assembled toads take a last practice opportunity.

The animals and birds have been given general charge of outside security this day. Jordy has turned over his guard duty at the entrance of Twith Mansion to Lupus. Crusty and Tuwhit have organized various bird patrols in the air above the Brook all the way to the outskirts of Squidgy's cottage. Bandy has the badgers stationed in the fields surrounding the farm.

Austin goes down to close the gate to the farm, and is almost swamped by the rush of animals coming from the Brook. Rabbits scurry up the path anxious to get the best viewing spot. Overhead, birds of all kinds hear the bell ringing and think they are late. There is chirping and chattering all along the various power and telephone lines.

Jared continues to call out his warning. "Half an hour to seven o'clock!"

WEDDING PRELUDE

Gumpa and gran'ma arrive fifteen minutes early. Gumpa, wearing Ernie's suit freshly cleaned for the occasion, has a small rosebud in his buttonhole to signify the joyful occasion. He is proud to represent the father of Taymar and Ambro and continues on up to the single chair on the hearth set out for him. Gran'ma stands just inside the door of the byre so she can coordinate things closer to the ceremony itself. As she welcomes the arriving guests, she looks more relaxed than she feels.

Uncle Andy and his family, dressed in their Sunday best, are already seated along the far wall of the sun porch. As others begin to arrive, they fall silent, apart from explanatory whispers by Uncle Andy.

Vyruss comes in with the choir and the musicians. They proceed to the back of the hearth and sit in the chairs provided for them. Vyruss was already wearing his best suit when he arrived back from Gyminge. He brought with him his gold cufflinks shaped like the woodlouses he loves. He had them specially made by the castle jeweler when he was the court physician. He only uses them on rare occasions, and they make him feel comfortably elegant. He also has a red rosebud in his buttonhole.

Vyruss is tuned in to the harmony of the occasion and desires to provide suitable background music throughout the procession. Sometimes it is a melody alone that soars like a lark over a silent meadow or a still lake instead of this very different setting. Sometimes it is the full choir, but often it is just a single soprano or tenor voice, or even a duet. Katie, his principal soprano, is equally free spirited and responsive to the atmosphere. They combine well together. Her sister, Gretchen, is no less talented and is the contralto soloist. Vyruss wonders whether they really need to go back to America at the end of the summer. There could well be a future for them in Gyminge.

The eight canopy bearers, all wearing their Sunday clothes, have not been needed on such a fine day. Micah leads them to the seats in the second row on the right.

Jordy escorts Queen Sheba to a front row seat on the left. She leaves the end seat vacant for her husband. Off in the distance she hears Jared ringing the bell indicating that Taymar and Ambro are leaving Twith Mansion.

The toad choir fills the air with new reverberating sound. They sing their hearts out as the wedding procession makes its way along the curving red carpet to the byre. Gerald, the two grooms and their attendants proceed slowly to the low and stately, even tragic, singing of the Bachelor's Lament which has happier words than the original.

When Gerald arrives, he walks confidently up the carpeted ramp to the hearth where he turns and stands central in front of the main table. He folds his hands in front, smiles at those present, and listens to the choir as he waits. His ponytail, neatly tied, is tucked underneath his robe. Rachael and Jenn excelled themselves in dressing him. He is superbly attired as Archbishop Crammer might have looked at the wedding of Henry VIII and Anne Boleyn. He has a beautiful white satin full-length cassock. A trim of gold braid decorates all the edges. His stole is deep crimson trimmed with gold. His miter is also white satin draped around a light wooden frame made by Stumpy to exactly fit the head size of the High Seer. It is almost a quarter of his full height and it ensures he is the male focal point. He is composed and not at all nervous.

A minute later, Ambro enters the byre. This is the interval at which Rachael is dispatching them from Twith Mansion. Barney is next and then Nick who is carrying a cream satin cushion with a solitary ring tied on with a bow matching Cymbeline's dress. They take their seats as instructed by gran'ma at the rehearsal.

Taymar, followed by Jock and then Lucas, walks down the aisle and goes to stand next to Gerald. Lucas carries the same cream satin cushion with a solitary ring tied on with a bow matching Elisheba's dress.

Gran'ma didn't dare have only one ring bearer for the two weddings. He would be sure to get things muddled. The two boys didn't bring any dress up clothes with them. Jock suggested they could borrow his kilts, but the boys downright refused to dress like girls. They also refused Jenn's offer to run up on the sewing machine some white satin suits with full cut sleeves and legs. Gran'ma picked up two matching sets of red bow ties, light blue shirts, and dark blue slacks for them in Ashford and hopes no one notices their shoes don't match.

Now the bridal procession begins to arrive. First is Titch wearing a short flouncy pink dress. She scatters rose petals from side to side in front of her as she walks, right up to where the brides will stand. By this time her basket of petals is empty. Her task is done, and she sits on the end of the first row on the right. Ginger feels very grown-up as she walks slowly down the aisle. It is her first time to be a maid of honor. The ginger-haired girl wears a full-length, mint green dress and carries a nosegay of yellow and white daisies. She proceeds to the end seat where Ambro and Barney sit at the back of the hearth.

Now Stumpy enters with Cymbeline. Ambro gasps and can hardly draw a breath. He swallows hard and there are tears in his eyes. Stumpy, too, feels that he has never seen his niece look so beautiful. Carrying a bouquet of red roses with long stems, she is simply radiant. Her full-length dress is pale yellow satin, almost a rich cream, overlaid with lace. It has a tight bodice, a straight skirt, and tight full-length sleeves pointed over the wrists to reach the back of each hand almost to the fingers. Her smooth-as-cream skin needs little makeup. Her lustrous brown hair, carefully coiffed by Jenn, falls in ringlets over her head and around her face. Her head is graced with a coronet of yellow daisies. There

KENNETH G. OLD & PATTY OLD WEST

is a suggestion of a veil in the net draped around the circlet, but it is only a suggestion and not a full veil. Her only adornment is the ruby necklace she received from Ambro's mother. Taymar had pressed it into her hand those many years ago as Tuwhit took them away from the battle developing around them to go warn King Rufus of the Wozzle invasion.

Stumpy is resplendent in the new clothes his niece made for him, With immense pride and unusual stateliness, he escorts Cymbeline down the aisle. He has completely forgotten that his leg hurts. As they pass Titch, she flashes them a smile. This is all so exciting! She wishes she still had rose petals to scatter. Reaching the hearth, Cymbeline sits next to her maid of honor, and Stumpy seats himself between his niece and Ambro.

There is a brief pause before Elisheba's maid of honor, Stormy, arrives. She is clothed in a lovely lavender, full-length dress. Like Ginger, she carries a nosegay of yellow and white daisies. She walks serenely up the ramp and stands to Gerald's far right.

All eyes turn to the entrance as Vyruss brings his baton down for the musicians to play Mendelssohn's Wedding March. Only Gumpa knows that it was written in 1842 for Shakespeare's play, *A Midsummer Night's Dream.*

WEDDINGS UNDERWAY

As Cydlo and Elisheba step through the door, Queen Sheba rises to her feet. The entire congregation stands watching as the king escorts the princess down the aisle to her waiting groom. Taymar's eyes widen and his mouth drops open at the sight of his beautiful bride. He quickly closes it as a broad grin stretches from ear to ear. He has difficulty standing still. He wants to run and embrace her.

Elisheba's green eyes dance with happiness. Her open-air country complexion needs no rouge on her rosy cheeks. The natural curls of her auburn hair fall in a tumble to her shoulders. Her royal blue chiffon dress has a scalloped neckline. The bodice is fastened with pearl buttons. The very full skirt falls to within a trace of the floor. It is decorated with tiny sky blue bows scattered in random profusion. Under the lights that Uncle Andy hung with such care, the sapphires encircling her coronet sparkle like a tumbling waterfall cascading around her. She carries a bouquet of long-stemmed yellow roses.

While all eyes are on Elisheba, gran'ma and Micah, almost unnoticed, slip quietly in and sit in the right-hand front row next to Titch.

Earlier, Cydlo was firm and resolved that he would wear his best woodsman's clothes for the wedding. He had firmly declined gran'ma's suggestions of apparel like Henry VIII, Lord Nelson, or a Beefeater. He did allow that he would carry his sword but not his shield. However, that was before his wife, Queen Sheba, arrived.

She was horrified. "How can you possibly think of failing your own daughter in such a way on her wedding day?"

His resistance was weakened, and he succumbed to her persuasions. Reluctantly, he agreed to trust his wife's judgment.

He did not know until this morning what she would produce for him to wear. By then it was too late to have qualms.

Queen Sheba herself is not an accomplished seamstress, but she can motivate others. Elisheba's own dress was completed, so she could help with her father's clothes. The princess was well schooled by Nettie. Cymbeline has made the clothes for her men folk through the centuries and worked alongside. The three of them selected the King of Hearts from a pack of cards as the model for the king's attire.

It suits him. On his head is the crown that Bimbo recovered from the shelf in the cave-tunnel. His new shoes with silver buckles were made by Gerald in response to an urgent request from gran'ma even before the queen herself arrived on the scene. His short, black tunic is heavily decorated with gold braid and bears the Gyminge crest of a rampant horse, a crouching lion, and a crown. He wears a broad gold sash on his left shoulder. His britches and full-length stockings are black. Around his waist, but hidden by his tunic, is his belt from which hang his sword in its scabbard and his dirk. For this occasion, the two weapons are reversed. The scabbard hangs to his right side and his dirk to his left side. The father of the bride did not need to be concerned about what he had to wear. All eyes are on the beautiful bride.

Cydlo, grave and regal, with Elisheba on his left arm, takes position facing Taymar and Jock. Elisheba hands her bouquet to Stormy.

Gerald quiets the congregation by raising his hands. His glorious apparel perfectly fits the occasion. Although this is his first time to perform a wedding ceremony, he is poised and relaxed. He gives the impression he has performed hundreds of similar ceremonies. He begins, "We will start with the Sharing of Secrets. I invite you, Taymar and Elisheba, to go sit in the high-backed chairs facing away from the congregation and share any final secrets you may have with each other. When you have done so, please raise your joined hands."

The congregation realizes how important this time is. They wait patiently while this quiet conversation takes place. It is a time for the members of the congregation themselves to remember and review their own marriages and what has followed.

While waiting, the High Seer takes from the larger table the items needed for the ceremony of the Two Eggs. He places them on the smaller table in the center.

The young couple in the high-backed chairs finished long ago and are just waiting until Gerald's movements cease. They look across at Gumpa who is the only one they can see. He signals to them with a nod, and they raise their clasped hands. They go back to where they were standing before.

The choir, humming softly, softens to silence.

Gerald stands in front of the table. "Please turn and face each other."

He addresses Taymar. "Are you free to marry this woman?"

Taymar replies clearly and positively. "Yes, I am."

He asks Elisheba a similar question and she responds with a loud, "Yes!"

He asks them both. "Do you wish to marry each other?"

Silly question. They grin broadly as they answer in unison, "Yes!"

He asks Taymar. "Do you have any secrets from your past life or your present that you have not shared with Elisheba?"

Taymar answers, "No."

He asks Elisheba, "Do you have any secrets from your past life, or your present, that you have not shared with Taymar?"

Elisheba shakes her head. "No."

Gerald addresses the congregation, "Do you agree that this couple can and should be allowed to marry?"

The congregation, including the choir, gives a resounding, "Yes!" as loudly as it is able. Even the full-size Beyonders, prompted by Uncle Andy, say, "Yes!"

Turning towards Elisheba, he asks, "Who gives this woman to be Taymar's bride?"

Cydlo's voice is loud and clear as he says, "I, her father, do so." There are tears in his eyes as he looks at his radiant daughter. Taking her right hand, he lifts it to his lips and kisses it in farewell before placing it in Taymar's outstretched left hand. As he does so, he whispers what his heart tells him. "Take good care of her, my son." He turns and walks slowly down the ramp to take the empty place beside his wife in the front row. They clasp hands tightly and are too choked by emotion to be able to say anything except with their eyes.

Gerald now moves to the rear of the table and beckons Taymar and Elisheba to face each other across it. "We will now symbolize the coming together of two individuals into the unity of a married couple. This goblet is empty." Gerald demonstrates by turning it upside down. "It is not a large goblet but this goblet will be a constant reminder to both Taymar and Elisheba of this day. Taymar, please select an egg and break it into the goblet."

It is a serious moment. There is no stirring or fidgeting or coughing anywhere.

Taymar picks up the nearest of the large brown eggs, fresh laid today by one of Max's chickens. He strikes the shell sharply with the back edge of the knife and breaks the two halves apart. It is a clean break. The egg, yolk and white, spills into the goblet. The three closest who can readily see what has happened break into smiles. Taymar's face tells all. The yolk is unbroken. Halfway there.

"Elisheba, will you now select an egg and break it into the goblet also?"

The girl is relaxed and confident. For hundreds of years she has been housekeeper to her father in Blindhouse Wood. Eggs are a familiar and regular part of her housekeeping.

Queen Sheba is remembering her own marriage to the man beside her. They had the same ceremony, but in very different circumstances. She squeezes her husband's hand tightly as she watches her daughter.

The princess takes an egg and, like Taymar, strikes it with the back of the knife and empties the contents into the goblet. As she puts the empty shells on the saucer, their smiles tell all.

Gerald lifts up the glass for all to see. Everyone is pleased to see two separate yolks in the goblet floating in the clear albumen. The unbroken yolks are taken to be a sign of the smoothness of the marriage in years ahead.

TAYMAR AND ELISHEBA

The recently appointed High Seer of Gyminge now gives his address to the couple. The congregation and the choir settle back in their seats. He explains, "The blending of these two eggs into the glass goblet is a symbol of your marriage. The yolks represent the two of you as separate individuals. They are still identifiable, and you still retain your own special characteristics. But the albumen has flowed into a common liquid that can no longer be separated. It is the same for the two of you. By your own choice, you have given up your separate, individual lives to become one half of a couple.

"Now the union will be sealed. The goblet will be placed into a container of near boiling water. As the albumen turns white, the differences within, although they are not destroyed, are lost to sight. Something totally new which did not previously exist, has been created. Going back from this present event will never be possible."

He carries the goblet back to Gumpa for the sealing. The carafe of steaming water is kept hot by the wicks of a little oil burner. Gumpa places the goblet carefully into a wire basket. It has been purpose made by Jordy to hold this particular goblet. As he submerges the basket into the near boiling water, the hot bubbling water rises up two thirds of its side.

There is complete silence in the byre. Vyruss has to fight back a desire to burst into song because gran'ma has insisted this particular moment deserves silence, not song.

Taymar and Elisheba hold hands across the table and watch, with all the congregation, as the translucent albumen slowly changes color and turns white.

Gumpa makes sure the eggs are well boiled before he removes the carafe from the burner and places a small bowl of wax over the flame to melt. When the goblet is cool enough to handle, he removes it from the carafe and pours half the liquid wax over the surface in the goblet. Slowly the wax solidifies. He replaces the carafe on the burner. The water needs to be near boiling for the next wedding.

While Gumpa is busy with sealing the eggs, Gerald removes the bowl of eggs, the saucer of egg shells, and the knife and places them on the table to the rear. They have served their purpose for this particular wedding. Only two embroidered towels and gran'ma's Waterford crystal bowl filled with warm water remain. Each towel has been lovingly embroidered by Vickie with a brown and white spaniel standing guard at a gate. It will forever remind them of the sacrifice Ollie made for them by attacking the SnuggleWump in the battle at the farmhouse.

When Gerald is satisfied that the ceremony of the Two Eggs is complete, he announces, "It is now time for the ceremony of Joined Hands. Taymar, please place your right hand in the water."

He does so.

"Elisheba, please place your left hand in the water and grasp hold of Taymar's hand."

As she does so, he continues, "The water symbolizes truth and love. Your linked hands represent the unity of your whole bodies immersed in truth and love so there is nothing untouched by it. Now please join your other hands above the table, making a ring. This symbolizes your unity in the world you live in. From this point forward, you will be known as one, not two. You will have the unity and strength of a ring to resist the pressures that will arise against you. You will become stronger by your union than you ever were as two individuals."

Gerald places his two hands on the shoulders of the groom and his bride. "I ask blessings on this couple in the name of all that is good and clean and pure and lovely and eternal. May they see out the days of their married lives back in the land that is their own. You may now dry each other's hands."

First Taymar dries Elisheba's hand, and then his bride does the same for him. Taymar recognizes the significance of the embroidery on the towel. The spaniel gave his life in defense of the Twith. A great surge of sadness and then appreciation for the Beyonders on the farm sweeps through him. He will explain the tears in his eyes to Elisheba later. The two small towels will be wedding keepsakes, not only of cleanliness and purity, but of an faithful dog's courage on a hectic night at the farmhouse.

It remains for Gerald to declare the couple husband and wife. "Before I declare you husband and wife, I ask you once again. Taymar, will you take this woman to be your wife for as long as you shall live? And will you love and cherish her all her days, come-what-may?"

Taymar replies solemnly, "I will."

"Elisheba, will you take this man to be your husband for as long as you shall live? And will you love and cherish him all his days, come-what-may?"

Elisheba looks at Taymar with love in her eyes as she answers quietly, "I will."

"Taymar as a symbol of this promise between you, do you have a ring you would like to place on your wife's finger?"

During the ceremony of the joined hands, Jock quietly removed the ring from Lucas's ring cushion. He carefully untied the bow while keeping one finger on the ring to prevent it from falling. He has been holding it on his own little finger, and he passes it to Taymar.

Taymar was not farsighted about a ring. He had a bracelet made but not a ring. In the Beyond there is no one who can make rings small enough to fit a Twith finger. Although, if he had thought about it, a ring could have been made Beyonder-size and then it could have been shrunk by shrinking a Beyonder holding it. However, Queen Sheba has allowed her daughter to choose from among the rings the wizard so conveniently sent with Dr.

Tyfuss. It has a narrow gold band and a single large amethyst held by six tiny claws. Taymar slips the ring on to his bride's left hand and it fits her finger perfectly.

Gerald intones, "I declare you, Taymar, and you, Princess Alicia, husband and wife. Taymar, you may kiss the bride."

AMBRO AND CYMBELINE

The newly married couple, freshly kissed, steps around Gerald. Not for them the stately walk arm in arm to the celebration waiting outside. They happily yield the focus to the new couple waiting to replace them. Taymar and Elisheba are followed by Jock, Lucas, and Stormy as they walk back and sit in the chairs being vacated by Ambro and Cymbeline and their attendants.

Gerald waits for the choir to complete its interval anthem. This has short solo parts for both Vyruss and Katie composed by the ambassador from Gyminge after breakfast this morning.

Responding to a beckoning nod from Gerald, Cymbeline gives her bouquet of red roses to Ginger. Stumpy takes his whispered cue from gran'ma and stands to Cymbeline's right. He takes his example from Cydlo and walks just as proudly as a king. For these few moments, he feels like a king standing beside a beautiful princess. With a welcoming smile, Cymbeline places her hand on his left elbow.

Gerald announces the Sharing of Secrets. While the new couple take their turn talking in the high-backed chairs, the High Seer replaces the various items on the front table. The hand towels have similar embroidery but are pale yellow rather than white. To avoid possible confusion, the goblet for the eggs has a different pattern.

Ambro and Cymbeline are living only for the moment, looking happily at each other. They, and those in the congregation who know them well, are reflecting on the long intervening years of separation, near despair and hopelessness as neither knew whether they would ever see each other again or even if the other was still alive or not. Theirs is a love that has lasted more than a thousand years. They have no secrets left to share so, instead of talking, each is reminiscing.

Ambro recalls his many years of imprisonment in the glass bottle. Twice he tried to escape but was recaptured. He never lost hope of being free however. When Bimbo and Bollin went on their secret quest, they helped him escape. Along the way they mentioned Cymbeline and his heart leapt with joy. He had spent many lonely hours wondering if he would ever see her again. Now, here he is, about to take her as his wife. He flashes a loving smile at her.

Cymbeline is also remembering the long years since she last saw Ambro. It was the day the battle for Gyminge began. That afternoon Ambro had told her he was going to ask his father for permission to marry her. She was fearful they had chosen someone else for him to marry, but he was certain they had not. That evening she and five others escaped to the Beyond. She had nearly lost hope of ever seeing him again and now, here they are, about to be married! What a wonderful day! She returns his smile with one of her own.

The quiet couple notices Gumpa nodding at them and raise their clasped hands high.

As they resume their former places, Gerald asks them to face each other. He asks them the same questions, instructing them to answer them thoughtfully and clearly.

They each answer a firm "No" to Gerald's question whether they have kept any secrets from each other. They have been talking almost nonstop for two weeks. There is nothing they have forgotten to talk about.

The congregation has no doubt that the couple can and should marry. Now comes Stumpy's moment. This is hard for him. Life will not be the same for him or for Barney. He dearly loves this girl who looks at him with such a sparkle in her brown eyes. Gerald asks, "Who gives this woman to be Ambro's bride?"

Stumpy gulps, hesitates only a moment, and answers loudly "I, her uncle and her guardian, do." His voice falters at the end. The old man looks across at his niece. His lip quivers and his eyes begin to water. He reminds himself, *This is a happy occasion.* But tears stream down his face, and he can do nothing about it. He tries to console himself. *At least I managed to say my piece, but only just.*

Impulsively Cymbeline turns to her uncle who has always been there for her. He has been both father and mother to her. She breaks into sobbing herself. They hold each other tightly.

The only other person to move is Barney. He recognizes his uncle's distress, takes hold of his hand, and leads him to his seat next to Titch. The little girl reaches over and grabs his hand, giving it a hard squeeze.

Gerald passes one of the hand towels to Cymbeline, stands behind the table and waits until she is again fully composed. No one else has moved. The girl smiles, dries her eyes and smiles again, first at Ambro and then at Gerald. She is ready again.

It is the ceremony of the Two Eggs. Gran'ma is thinking, *This is a part of the Twith ceremony I would have liked in my wedding to Gumpa. I wonder, though, could he have managed an unbroken yolk? Probably, and knowing him, the egg he chose would have a double yolk!* She smiles at her husband who is hoping the water will be hot enough to cook the egg whites and has no idea what his wife is thinking.

Ambro and Cymbeline both achieve unbroken yolks. Gerald holds the goblet high. He makes a similar address to his earlier one, emphasizing a new unity come into being before the eyes of all present. He takes the goblet back to Gumpa who is relieved when before long he sees a change of color developing.

Ambro and Cymbeline only half watch the eggs. The majority of the time they steal glances at each other.

Gerald is busy sorting out his table for the ceremony of Joined Hands. As the couple join hands in the bowl of water and join their free hands over the bowl, Barney gets ready for the last part of the ceremony. Per gran'ma's instructions, he keeps one finger on the ring while he unties the bow and removes the ring from Nick's ring cushion.

Cymbeline generously gave up the ring she once thought she would use at her wedding so Elisheba would have an engagement ring. Queen Sheba has allowed Cymbeline to choose one of hers from the rings the wizard sent. It is not a difficult choice for the girl. Several rings have larger stones, but the ring she chooses is a perfect match in color to the ruby in her necklace. Central in the narrow gold band, the ruby is held with four small gold claws. Two small diamonds are on either side.

As Ambro slips the ring on Cymbeline's finger, Julie's husband, Max, blinks and rubs his eyes. He has never before been able to see the Twith. He blinks again and reaches out to hold tight onto his wife's hand. Something wonderful has happened. He whispers to her, "I can see what your father is describing! At last, after all these years, I can really see the Little People!" It is a miraculous day indeed.

The two weddings are almost over and Micah is glad. He is anxious to have this part done with so the reception can get underway. There are many mouth-watering delicacies on offer and the smell of all the food being prepared has been tantalizing his nostrils all afternoon.

The animals waiting outside, especially the rabbits, are also ready for the festivities to start. The toads plan to exercise their vocal chords to the full. There is a promise of a Raisin-Fest and all the birds and animals are looking forward to that.

It is not that long before the sounds of the recessional can be heard. Let the celebrations begin!

SQUIDGY'S COTTAGE

Griselda Squidge made her way to the post office first thing this morning. She makes the daily trek into the village in the vain hope of receiving a letter from the wizard. She rarely gets any mail. The only other person who ever corresponds with her is her sister. Now that she is part of the famous Penwith Nancarrow West-Country Travelling Circus, she no longer has time to write.

Squidgy was pleasantly surprised when the post mistress handed her a letter. *Oh, dear Griswold finally wrote to apologize for departing so suddenly without even saying goodbye.* Looking at the return address, she is further surprised. It reads simply: Pansy Nancarrow. It is postmarked St. Newlyn East. Penwith has taken his circus back to Cornwall. No surprise there, but to see his surname after Pansy's means he and Oolagoola must have adopted her. They have no idea that she is Squidgy's middle-aged sister, Frijji. The wizard transformed her into a schoolgirl so she could infiltrate the farmhouse and spy for him. When the circus arrived to give special performances at the farm, she decided to remain a schoolgirl and joined the circus as the target for Oolagoola's knife throwing act.

When Squidgy gets back to her cottage, she makes herself a pot of tea and settles down in her rocking chair to read Frijji's letter. The salutation *Dear older sister* makes her harrumph. "I'm not that much older than she is!" She continues reading.

> *Penwith and Oolagoola are like father and mother to me. I share a caravan with the trapeze artist. She plans to leave at the end of this summer tour and is teaching me everything she knows before then. It means that I am likely to take over as the star of the trapeze. I'm not at all frightened of the heights and I absolutely love the excitement and hearing the crowds ooh and aah.*

It was thoughtful of you to send Growler to find me, but my dear Great Dane is not adjusting well to circus life. Even the lions are afraid of him, and he made an enemy of Penwith when he bit his star elephant. So he has to be kept in a cage most of the time. However, he has a good friendship with Moley.

Mrs. Squidge has a twinge of guilt about the former mole king. "It was my yeast buns—the same ones that changed Max's chickens into titchy teros—that transformed Moley into a zebra striped duck-billed platypus. The wizard made a weightlifter out of him and gave him the magnificent name of The Masked Menace from Madagascar."

She goes back to reading the letter.

Moley sends his greetings. No one has beaten him at weightlifting yet.

Actually, Penwith would like to talk to you about joining the circus also. I'm not joking, I'm absolutely serious. To start with, we could probably live together and share the caravan I'm in. There'll be extra space when the other girl leaves. In the long-term, though, you would probably want your own place.

Griselda snorts as she reads. "There is no likelihood the two of us could live together in a caravan for long, but I wonder why Penwith would want me to join his circus?"

She reads further to see if Frijji says why.

Penwith is interested in the SnuggleWump. No other circus in the world has a SnuggleWump. It could make him the top circus in England. You need to take good care of him, sis. He could be worth his weight in gold. He doesn't need to lose any more ears though. There is a spare tiger cage that is made to measure for the SnuggleWump to live in.

Penwith is also interested in the teros, but he feels they are a bit small. It would be difficult for the patrons to see them flying around a huge circus tent. They would be hard to keep track of. Could they possibly be enlarged to say the size of cows? Then they, too, really would have a future. People talk about flying cows, but no one has ever seen one. What a combination! Flying cows and a SnuggleWump! Can you work on that? You really do have a gift with yeast buns, and it shouldn't be beyond your abilities.

Penwith would engage you as the tamer and your animals would be part of the same contract. It could all work out very well, and maybe he would even let you help with the accounts. I know that you have always had a good head for figures.

Again, Squidgy snorts. "I'm not interested in doing Penwith's accounts for him! I'll stick to managing my own accounts, thank you."

The circus is moving on towards Brighton, stopping on the outskirts of the bigger villages along the way. Penwith plans to have a final circuit of the southeast before heading back west to Cornwall for the winter. If everything works out, we will come back to Rye in about a month's time for the festival week there. I hope I'll be able to see you then. Perhaps Griswold could come down and visit. It would be good to see him and express my appreciation for what he did for me.

By the way, how is your new broom working out? It's the newest high-speed model so I hope you've been able to keep it under control.

Love,
Frijji (now Pansy)

Squidgy thinks, *She has no idea how powerful that broom is!* She goes out and takes a long look at the SnuggleWump. The animal whimpers a greeting and wriggles his tail. She pats him on both heads. "Poor thing. It's a pity about those missing ears. I wonder if I could fashion a pair of false ones?" His missing

KENNETH G. OLD & PATTY OLD WEST

ears each left a wound when he lost them, but the wounds have healed well. However, his hearing is not like it used to be. His eyes remain a steady green. His necks are in frequent movement, and look like two snakes of a snake charmer harmonizing to the same reedy tune.

Although the creature gazes up at her with admiration, he grimaces. He has assorted aches and pains and wonders, *Am I beginning to get arthritis?*

The birds at the top of the ash tree watch him but no longer bother to report his activities back to the farmhouse.

On the ridge of the cottage, grouped close at one end, almost like a permanent decoration, are the six teros. They are content to have the roof to themselves without the distractions of either Rasputin or Cajjer. Since the excursion that their mistress made on her broomstick that almost brought her disaster, they are more than satisfied that she is less adventurous these days. She looks up at them. "I'm not even going to try enlarging them until I get them away from the ridge of my roof. Six cows on the roof are likely to bring about its collapse!"

The letter causes Griselda to ponder her own future. "Perhaps the time has come for me to think of leaving the Brook and launching out into a new line of activity more in line with my gifts. After all, I am getting on in age and it might soon be too late to launch into a new career. Now that I think about it, I really enjoyed the circus performance in the back field at the farm. The atmosphere of the crowded tent was exciting and made me feel like a schoolgirl again. My sister was excellent in her role as a circus performer. I'm sure I could do just as well. There is clearly strong dramatic talent in our family."

She goes inside, looks into the mirror, and tries twisting her face into a becoming smile. It doesn't work, and she tries the other side of her face.

"Don't worry, Cajjer," she calls out as she cracks an imaginary whip. "I'll take you with me if I go."

The contortions on her face and the swift downward motion of her arm startle the cat. He scoots out onto the porch scared out of his life. He is uncertain and fearful about what is happening to his mistress.

Squidgy hears Cajjer moaning from his prone position on the porch mat. She is oblivious to the fact that she has frightened him. "I'm a bit worried about Cajjer. He seems to blink much more than he used to. It's a relief to see that his swollen head is almost back to normal, but he shows little inclination to stray far from my side. And he still isn't really enjoying his saucer of bread and milk. Nor is he back to trying to catch birds."

She waits until the cool of the evening to go out and work in the garden. Down on her knees, she carries on a conversation with herself as she pulls at the weeds. "I need to let Griswold know about the offer I just received. He won't be happy, I don't think. He will lose this suitable location for keeping track of his enemies. However, he hasn't been in touch for some time. It's been at least three days." Sudden anxiety assaults her. "Perhaps he is ill. I need to get in touch with him, and inquire about his welfare. I'll write him a letter and seek his advice. No, that won't work. If I seek his advice, I'll be obliged to take it. It might not be what I want to do. I want to keep my options open. I'll just tell him I'm planning to join my sister in the circus and wait for his reaction."

She grumbles, "Why do I always have more weeds than anyone else?" With some relief she muses, "I wonder why all the rabbits are missing from my garden this evening? I almost always have to chase them away from my vegetables." She has little idea of the activities going on up at the farm.

The SnuggleWump also notices that the rabbits are not around. "I miss the friendly little creatures. They are somebody to talk to and more cheerful and less smelly than Jacko. I've noticed that he keeps going down to the bog looking at the orchids. He never picks any though. Just now he is indoors at Mole Hall.

Although I saw him go in earlier, he hasn't emerged since to even exchange the time of day. He used to keep asking when the wizard will be visiting next, but now he never even mentions his name."

As Griselda works away in her garden, she hears the steady burping of the toads singing at the wedding reception up at the farm. She would never have called it singing, but there is certainly a recognizable rhythm and beat to whatever is happening. She wonders, "Why are they so much louder than usual? Oddly, it rather reminds me of the singing of the choir at the chapel I used to attend before I met Mr. Squidge." She hums the first line of a familiar hymn.

Her thoughts lead her far from her present task of weeding her vegetables. *I wonder what the rascal is doing now? Well, I wish him ill whatever it is.* She chuckles wickedly as she expresses her thoughts. "It would give him a turn if I suddenly showed up at Fairfield in Newlyn East as a leading performer in the circus. I can see myself sparkling with spangles and resplendent in silver tights. It would be sure to embarrass him and that would serve him right! And the sweetshop girl as well."

Severely nasty thoughts cross her mind. *May all the meat in his butcher shop go bad and all the sausage skins be full of holes! And may the children of the village steal all her sweets!*

SPECS STUDIES THE LIGHT

The wedding reception in the garden at Gibbins Brook Farm is in full swing. Wedding cakes are cut, toasts are made, and speeches given. The guests mingle and congratulate the newlyweds. Vickie is excited to learn that her uncle Max is now able to see the Twith at last.

The celebrations continue with the Raisin-Fest for the toads and rejoicings with the other animals and birds. When the Brook creatures finally disperse, the festivities move indoors. Everyone quickly changes from their wedding finery into party clothes instead!

More music, skits, speeches, and dancing ranging from the sedate to the spectacular are soon underway. In spite of the efforts of the entertainment crew to keep to a schedule, much of what happens has not been previously rehearsed, but no one cares very much.

Dr. Tyfuss feels like one of the family. *I cannot remember when I've had such a good time. I will be sorry to depart tomorrow, and I'll make it as late as possible.*

In the atmosphere of general goodwill, Stormy tries to prevail upon Gumpa to open his present. "Gumpa, don't you think now would be a good time to open your gift?"

Gumpa is not yet ready to see what his package holds. "No, Stormy, this isn't the time for that. But I'll do so after breakfast. After the dishes have been washed and put away, of course. It will be something of a surprise for all of us to look forward to. How's that?"

Gran'ma is so delighted with the success of the weddings that she totally relaxes all the rules. Amazingly, she announces, "You children can go to bed whenever you like." A chorus of surprised cheers raises up at once. "The refreshments left over from the reception are laid out on the kitchen table if anyone wants them. In view of the late hour, we'll set breakfast for half past nine. As usual, the table preparation and cooking crews are to be on duty twenty minutes earlier. Bajjer will be the bell boy. For myself, I am off to seek my bed. I'll see you in the morning." She expects that Gumpa will follow her up the stairs and is surprised to see he does not.

Gumpa has a sudden burst of new energy. He tells her, "I'll stay up and see to the locking up and turning off the lights."

As it gets later and later, some of the children snatch forty winks in snuggle up places downstairs in the green or red rooms, unwilling to give up the festivities too early lest they miss something important.

Gumpa's burst of energy doesn't last all that long. Before long he shepherds the children off to bed. He calls out, "Lights off! Scurry yourselves on up to bed now."

Most of the children are too exhausted to complain.

Bajjer rings the bell vigorously shortly after eight-thirty. It is unnecessarily early, but he is eager to get the day started. Gumpa promised to open his gift after breakfast this morning. The church service at the Methodist Church, the nearest of the two churches, is not until eleven o'clock, but those who like to walk usually set out between a quarter after and half past ten depending on their intention to hurry, or dawdle by the wayside, or take the long way through the woods. There won't be much time for that today.

Specs arranged in advance with Gumpa to be excused early from the table. Last night, he asked Jock to bring both the king and Gerald upstairs for an early morning talk. He sees the three of them emerging from the staircase leading into the mansion, and doesn't wait for the others to finish working on their eggcups. He moves quickly across to the fireplace and carries the three tiny folk out to the sun porch. He pulls the door shut so that the table chatter will not disturb them. He has Jock shrink him to size, and will enlarge later to get his friends back to the mansion staircase.

They make themselves comfortable on the settee. Specs notices the king is wearing his ring and it is glowing with its usual warm red light. Before the weddings, the schoolboy searched through Gumpa's encyclopedias and used gran'ma's computer to find out a little more about the ring and its light. He has waited patiently until after the wedding celebrations to share his discoveries. This is the first opportunity he has had. He wants Jock and Gerald present because he will not only talk about the ring but about light itself and about seeing into the future.

The boy clears his throat and nervously adjusts his spectacles. "We have been puzzling about the light in the ring, how it might possibly work, and how it can help us. Why does it glow when Cydlo wears it, but not when anyone else wears it? If there is power in the light of the ring, what is it? Can we find out how to use it?

"I don't have those answers but I want to share about the mysterious aspects of light that I found out so far. I don't really understand all that I've read. There are lots of words I don't understand, and some of them are quite long. But everything I have to talk about is very, very tiny.

"Almost the smallest things that exist are called atoms. Think of the smallest thing you can think of and then divide its size by a million. That might get close to the size of an atom. Different objects have different atoms. Various atoms mixed together create molecules. Molecules combined together in great numbers become big enough to see. Things like water, cheese, and strawberry jam are made up of molecules. Everything we can touch, taste, feel, or see contain atoms merged into molecules.

"But even smaller than the atoms are its parts. In the normal tiny center of the atom are a certain special number of protons. Whizzing continuously around them are an equal number of electrons. And in all the atoms except one, there are other little bits called neutrons. Those are almost as heavy as protons. When we pick up something heavy, the weight is mostly the millions and millions of protons and neutrons. The electrons weigh almost nothing.

"There is also another little oddity and that may be what we see in the king's ruby. It is called a photon and probably doesn't weigh anything at all. It seems to be just bright light—light energy—radiating constantly and creating pulses.

"In a hundred years time, I think people will know a lot more about light than they do now. They still don't really know what light is. Light is not just a flat, straight line. Nor can it be explained simply by saying it is a wave. It is much more than that. There are various theories trying to explain all of light's various properties. Hardly any of them, though, account for everything that happens. Sometimes one kind of theory about light seems to work, and sometimes another. Light is like the two ends of a seesaw. It seems to be either in waves or in lots and lots of tiny impulses called photons knocking around close to each other. These have energy and energy means power.

"Most light tends to diffuse itself, which means the light tends to spread out immediately in every direction it can. If it is blocked off with a brick wall, it can't go through and it stops diffusing. It lights up one side of the wall and the other side is dark.

"We can imagine that the light of the sun or the moon doesn't just come towards the earth we live on, but goes out in all directions, as much away from the earth as towards it. Something like the way noise goes in all directions when we shout.

"One more new word I learned is ions. They are atoms with unbalanced electrons—either more or less—and that means it carries either a positive or negative electric charge. Magnets have this kind of charge. When you put them together, they either stick to each other or back away from each other. Sometimes the ion itself is a single free electron and nothing else. When a ruby—loaded with ions—is in some way excited by an external source of energy, it produces an intense beam of red light. Other materials produce different effects and colors.

"You notice both Gumpa and gran'ma wear glasses, and so do Gerald and I. It's because our eyes are not perfect. The lenses of our glasses bend the light that comes through them. That's called refraction. The corrections enable all of us to see better.

"There is a type of eye surgery that involves the use of a knife. If Gerald were doing an operation, he would use a steel knife for cutting. But there is another kind of operation to improve vision called Lasik surgery. Instead of using a knife, a blade of light called a laser is used to do the cutting. The first laser was created in 1960 by shining a high-power flash lamp on a ruby! Interesting, isn't it, that it was a ruby.

"Lasers work by adding energy to atoms or molecules, so that there are more in a high-energy, or excited, state than in some lower-energy state. Scientists and inventors use various kinds of mechanisms to stir up the ions in a crystal. Sometimes two parallel mirrors are used to bounce the light to and fro and this does the trick although it is not the only way. The excited light rays are no longer diffused but become a small narrow beam of light with intense energy. It can even burn. However, there are also some cold lasers. The laser can be pointed and aimed to travel either very short, measured distances, or great distances.

"Now, just suppose that for the king's ring, Cydlo is the energy source that excites the light into this new shape."

The three Twith are listening intently. They try desperately to understand what Specs is getting at. Questions from Jock and Gerald fly fast and furious, not waiting for answers.

"Cun th' ring indeed prove ta be a sword or a knife? Is tha' possible? Does i' e'er becum blunt?"

"What all can it cut through? Can it cut through a fog? Or glass? Or rock? How long does it last?"

"Ye say i' cun extend long distances. 'Ow far?"

"Can Cydlo learn how to make a blade of light? It has never happened with the ring before, why should we expect it to happen now?"

The king, without comment, holds up his hand so all four of them can see the ring easily. They look carefully. The light is bright and diffused throughout the rubies in the ring. The red light does wax and wane; they have observed this previously. Sometimes the light is brighter than at other times. Somehow the king needs to stir up—or excite—the light in the rubies in the ring. If the photons can be organized into a narrow strip of intense and powerful light that can burn or cut, then the chances for the success of the Return improve immensely.

Specs continues, urgent and intense. "Surely this is the fulfillment of Dayko's vision about the restraint of the king. I am sure it is possible, although I can't tell you how to do it, that the light in the ring can surely cut the curtain into pieces. And that will allow the salt wind from the south to blow over the land ending the restraint of the king. What else can possibly do it?

"It will mean so many other things too. It will mean the certain defeat of the wizard once the birds, and even the animals of the Brook, can go straight over into Gyminge and take part in the battle against the goblin soldiers.

"As you said, it has never happened before with the ring. That doesn't mean that it can't happen. None of the previous verses happened before either. The qualities of light that permitted the laser beam to be discovered always existed. It just took the fullness of time during this past fifty years for it to happen. There had to be someone who could find out how to do it. Perhaps this is why the Return has been delayed until now!

"Almost everything else that the Rime has foretold has now happened except for the salt wind. Earlier we thought that line had been fulfilled, but without the full stop at the end of that line, it has not yet happened the way Dayko envisioned. Dr. Tyfuss raised the black and white flag, even the brides have processed to the byre. What's left is that our journey back has to begin at the waterfall and lead on to the wall and one of us children will lead on to the prize—Gyminge Castle. That's all that's left and all of that is in Gyminge, not on the Brook."

Specs smiles at his companions. They will need to think through what he has been saying. "If Jock will be good enough to enlarge me, I will carry you back to the mansion staircase."

CHAOS AT THE TABLE

Specs is still out on the porch with the three Twith. The clean-up squad is finished with their duties and everyone crowds back around the table anxious to watch Gumpa open his gift. It sits in front of him on the empty table top. The glittering gift package is addressed simply, *'To Gumpa with love'*. He looks up and around the clustered faces smiling at him. He is amused at all the attention this little gold package that arrived out of the blue is receiving.

Aside from wondering what is inside, part of the children's interest lies in the mystery of the sender. None of the children has owned up to it, but Gumpa is certain that one of them is behind this. He thinks, *If this is a trick, there will be a little giveaway smirk on one of these faces.* He looks around at the children again. *I don't detect one yet. Well, I'll know soon enough.*

The small, gold cube measures approximately four inches on each side. Gran'ma asks, although she knows he is going to refuse, "Do you want to use a pair of my scissors to cut the ribbon?"

Gumpa shakes his head. "No, thank you. I can manage." He carefully removes the silver ribbon and bow and works to untie the knots in the string.

Gran'ma looks at her watch, but her husband is not going to be hurried.

Carefully, he unfolds the wrapping paper without tearing it.

The children recognize the gift for what it is the moment they see the green top and the winding handle on one side. Multiple shouts of "It's a Jack-in-the-Box! A Jack-in-the-Box!" reverberate around the room. The sides of the box alternate red and green.

Gumpa stares at the contraption. It is obvious that he needs some instruction.

"You have to turn the handle to open the lid, Gumpa, and then the Jack will jump out of the box." The heads crowd closer.

Gumpa looks around for approval as he takes hold of the crank handle and turns. The box plays a tinny tune that the children recognize instantly. They all begin to sing along with the music.

All around the mulberry bush
The monkey chased the weasel
The monkey thought 'twas all in fun
Pop ....!

A clown with a blue hat springs out of the box with great force as though he is heading for the attic! His two red arms are bouncing and swinging. As he is pulled to a shuddering halt by the restraint of the spring, the concoction in the clown's hat keeps on going. The powder that was so carefully prepared in the castle laboratory at Gyminge, scatters all over everything nearby.

In a split instant there is total chaos. The children scream in terror as they fan the black ash away from their faces. Not only have the mumps, measles and chickenpox germs exploded everywhere, but so have the itching and sneezing powders, and the blackness powder. A great wave of darkness billows like smoke from a blazing oil fire across the room, into the kitchen, and up the stairs. As Specs, with the three Twith in his hand, opens the porch door and rushes in to see what the screaming is all about, they, too, are covered with the dust.

Gran'ma closes her eyes tight and yells instructions, "Get outside, quick! Go on outside! Hurry! Open the doors! Open the windows!" She gathers a couple of the nearest children under her apron, trying to shield them. The older children try to help the younger ones nearest to them. But it is so dark that no one can see which way to run outside. They are bumping and jostling into each other. Gumpa struggles towards the birdhouse window to try to throw the unwanted gift out into the open air, but he can't see the children in his way. They are jumping, pushing, beating the air, coughing, sneezing, choking, and itching themselves like crazy.

Downstairs in Twith Mansion, the other Little People, including Vyruss, are trying to keep the invading clouds of darkness locked back in the passage by sealing the curtain with their hands and feet. They have no idea what is happening upstairs, although they can hear the noises of panic. The darkness is even coming through the curtain fabric and the lighted walls of the mansion grow dim. Barney runs to open the doors to the outside.

By now the darkness upstairs is so intense that no light shines anywhere. There is no light coming in from any of the windows or glazed doors. It is darkness like the plague in Egypt! Except! Except for the light from the ring on Cydlo's finger! What is happening? The only thing it is possible to see through the prevailing gloom is the faint red glow from the ring. Everything else is completely blotted out.

Specs yells to his three passengers, "Hold on! Hold on *tight!* I'm going to lift you up high." He stands on the threshold of the door to the porch and holds his hand up high above his head. "Use the ring, Cydlo, use the ring!" Something starts to happen and there is no explaining what or why. The king points his ring towards the center of the room and the light gains strength. The darkness, the awful blackness of total darkness, changes slowly from black to red. The two colors are locked in some kind of struggle, and the red is gaining. The red light has never been so bright and moment by moment the brightness increases. Within the darkness shadows of movement begin to be discernible. The sense of panic and turmoil begins to ease.

Specs knows everything depends on the king and the ring. He moves to the center of the room, where the darkness is most intense. His voice is louder than Cydlo's and he calls out instructions. "Look towards me, everybody! Look towards me! If you can't see me, look towards my voice."

The room becomes bathed in the red light. Now the coughing and choking are diminishing, and the sneezing is less frequent. The eyes are smarting less, the throats less painful, and the awful itchiness eases. The red light, diffused and glowing brightly, continues to gain over the blackness. Slowly, very slowly, individuals begin to emerge from within the darkness. Gumpa gets near enough at last to pitch the Jack-in-the-Box outside. One by one, the windows are thrown open. Micah runs to open the front door, and then flings open the two porch doors to the outside. Fresh air begins to blow through.

Specs is anxious that not a single corner of darkness shall remain. He knows enough to realize that the light has somehow defeated the darkness. Now they must not allow the darkness any remaining foothold in the house lest it reassert itself. This is again some unexpected shenanigan of the wizard, and if it weren't for the ring, he would have won the contest. As Specs moves from room to room, Jock and Gerald sit down and steady Cydlo against falling. First it is down into the mansion, and then it is the turn of each room in the farmhouse to be bathed in the red light of the ring. They start in the attic, down to the bedrooms, then back to the downstairs rooms, including the porch and the pantry.

The light, ordinary precious daylight, streams back into the house, but something strange now happens to the light in the ring. Specs lowers his hand so that he can see better. The bright, diffused light that vanquished the darkness and relieved the discomfort of the children, is focusing itself into a solid beam of light.

Specs realizes what is happening although he doesn't know why. He can see danger. He cries, "Cydlo, be careful where you point the light. Point the light upwards." Carefully keeping his hand level, he hurries out to the porch. The narrow beam of light from the ring hits the translucent plastic panels that comprise the roof of the porch. Suddenly, a wiggly cut piece of the roofing drops onto the settee and bounces to a stop. Specs calls out desperately, anxious to preserve the rest of the roof, "Take off the ring, Cydlo! Take it off now!" Somehow, he doesn't know how, the ring has become a laser and it needs to be brought under control before more damage is done!

The children have now almost recovered from the attacks of coughing and itching and sneezing, but are much less inclined to activity than usual. They have been seriously frightened and there is an underlying worry that the wizard might not yet be finished with his mischief.

Neither gran'ma nor Queen Sheba intends to have any residue of the Jack-in-the-Box hanging around anywhere. Even Cydlo, Vyruss, and Gumpa have dusters thrust into their hands. Every available hand is needed for a thorough cleaning throughout both homes. Gran'ma feels the children need some energetic diversion from the frightening events of the morning!

The attic is having a working over it has rarely had in its five hundred years. Gran'ma herself is up there supervising. She recognizes the house has been needing a good cleaning anyway, and this is the opportunity to get it done. She is surprised at what emerges in the way of clutter and mess from underneath the boys' beds. There are four baskets of rubbish to throw away! She shakes her head and wonders, *How on earth can they live in such a mess?*

Stormy supervises the cleaning of the bedroom level and Jenn is in charge of the ground floor. The three outside doors are still open, and all the windows in the house are now wide open. The curtains are pulled fully back and blowing in a good breeze.

The frantic activity goes on past the usual lunchtime. Rachael and Titch have quickly prepared a simple meal of soup and sandwiches. Gumpa compliments them, "Well done, girls. You are mighty fine cooks."

◠

In the mansion lunch is already over. Vyruss is as puzzled as anyone by what happened this morning. He is thankful that no serious damage or injuries occurred except to the porch roof. Although the Jack-in-the-Box was clearly one of the wizard's tricks, no one has suggested that Vyruss might have anything to do with it. They do ask if he has any explanation how it came about, but he has no idea. That would be typical of the wizard, deceiving even his own servants. Had it succeeded, it could have completely destroyed any hope of the Return to Gyminge.

Vyruss expresses his own concerns. "I will have to return to Gyminge lest the wizard get suspicious that I have changed sides. Perhaps I can wait until teatime, though."

The Twith are in agreement. Buffo and Tuwhit are nearby outside and are alerted to be ready to take Dr. Tyfuss to the waterfall.

He is not going to get as far as he expects!

PRU AND NETTIE

In a quaint little cottage surrounded by trees on the west side of Blindhouse Wood in Gyminge, two elderly Twith women share a quiet life. It is not always completely quiet, however. Loopy, their brown-and-tan wolf-dog, barks her head off when chasing the rabbits away from the garden. All the creatures in the game know it is just noisy fun.

On occasion, there have been a few dramatic events occur in Pru's rather hum-drum days. Long, long ago Elisheba, fleeing from robbers, sought refuge for a short while. Pru sent Lupus, Loopy's brother, with the girl when she left in search of her father. Not long after that Elisheba's old nurse, Nettie, called in and was invited to stay on as a companion. They quickly became fast friends.

Then only a little over two weeks ago, two well-mannered young men stopped in. Bimbo and Scayper were seeking help in looking for a companion captured by Hardrada's robber gang. They were likeable young men, although Scayper's haircut left a lot to be desired. Pru asked Loopy to show them the way to the robbers' camp. She returned home happily with messages indicating their companion, Bollin, had been rescued, and all three were headed for a tunnel on the southern border and then through a waterfall back to the Beyond.

This particular summer morning, the two women each have something to share. Over breakfast they discover that each had a long dream during the night. To their great surprise, they had the same dream! They are too wise to ignore this. To dream the same dream must have some deeper meaning than the usual casual jumble of housekeeping images. They think back over yesterday. They can't recall that anything in their conversations or what they did was likely to trigger such a dream. There must be more to it.

Pru, who has something of the seer's gift for seeing into the future, listens attentively as Nettie dredges her mind for even the tiniest details that she didn't previously mention as she repeats what she remembers of her dream. "Both of the young men, Bimbo and Scayper, were dressed exactly as they were on their visit to the cottage. It looked like Loopy was with them. They had many companions with them—men, women, boys, and girls. There were many more children than adults. Some were carrying weapons. They seemed to be involved in a fight with Hardrada.

"One among them looked like a peasant. He was a burly, bearded, redheaded man, and he was wearing a crown. One of the boys was carrying a flag. Some were carrying lighted torches. The whole group was excited and happy. Throughout the dream. there was the background sound of splashing water, but they were not wading through water. They were passing through what seemed to be a large, dark, dry tunnel. Suddenly there was the sound of a sharp explosion behind them followed by a deep rumble. As heads turned to look for the cause, there was a similar, but louder, sound all above and around them. The heavy rumble was falling rock, and they were caught in complete darkness. I woke up and rubbed my eyes wondering if the roof of the cottage had fallen in. Neither you nor I were part of the dream itself. I was merely an observer of events."

Pru asks, "Was one man wearing a woman's skirt? I remember seeing that."

"Yes, I forgot. I did see one wearing a red-and-black-and-yellow plaid skirt."

Pru suggests, "Let's leave the clearing of the table and washing up of the dishes for a while. We need to fathom out what the dream means. I think it is a warning of some kind. It is clearly not meant for us, but for our two recent visitors. What kind of trouble are they in? Did they get trapped in the tunnel they were headed towards when they left? But that was more than two weeks ago. They would surely be beyond the tunnel by now and well into the Beyond. I wonder how far into the Beyond they live? It could be many days walk, but I seem to remember that Bimbo indicated it was nearby. Do we need to do anything? If so, what?"

Loopy, who has been lying on the hearth between them, barks sharply twice. That is not her warning someone is approaching, it is merely to let them know that she has been listening to their conversation. She jumps to her feet and paces around the room restlessly. Her movements have clear meaning.

"Yes!" says Pru. "You are right, Loopy. We need to send you to warn them. It will be up to you to discover where they are. If anyone can find them you can. I'll write a letter to the two young men telling them about our dream. They must be very, very careful whenever they find themselves in a tunnel. Nettie, you write down our dream while I write the letter to go with it."

First, she adds more food to Loopy's bowl on the hearth. "Here, you better eat a little more. You may not get any food for quite a while."

The two women finish writing about the same time. Pru's handwriting is careful, elegant, well formed, although now a little shaky. Nettie's is more like a young girl's, written with a firm round hand.

Loopy has a special collar with a little envelope pouch for messages. It's not the first time she has carried a message, although it has been many centuries since she did so. The notes are placed in the pouch. Pru bends her head towards the dog as she fastens the collar, and gives some last instructions. "Loopy, they said they were heading for the tunnel at the border and then on to a waterfall. Now that means a river or a lake. Head east towards the sunrise. When you come to the very first river follow where it is flowing. It is sure to be going south and hopefully it will lead you to the waterfall. If you don't find a tunnel or a waterfall when it reaches the border, then cross over and try the next river.

"Be careful at the tunnel when you do find it. When you get through it, that's likely where the waterfall will be, and the water will be falling into the Beyond. From then on you are entirely on your own and you'll just have to do what seems best to you. We shall be waiting anxiously for you to return. Travel safely."

Loopy is highly cautious. She knows little of the larger conflict between the wizard and the Twith for her knowledge is limited to overheard snatches of conversation as she accompanied Bimbo and Scayper to Hardrada's robber camp. She knows, though, that the goblins are clearly enemies of the two boys and so is the goblin king, Haymun. Along with the goblins is another enemy—the wizard.

Rather than branching out diagonally across the fields towards the southeast, Loopy follows the flank of the woods and the path that fringes them. She is certain to eventually meet with a stream emerging from the woods and then she will follow it. There are no other travelers on the path, and no signs of rural life although the fields to her right are planted and well tended. She knows it will be a long journey, and sets into an easy loping pace. She does not pause to rest. If possible, she would like to be across into the Beyond before nightfall and find some hiding place in a wood or thicket until dawn. She is not going to let tomorrow bother her at this moment. Today has enough uncertainties.

The distance falls behind as her long, loping strides lead on to where she will encounter the stream from Gyminge Lake. Slowing to a walk, she sniffs the air. She stops and sniffs again. She smells, not only the water ahead, but a strange, strong, toad smell. She identifies it correctly, but cannot understand why she should be smelling toads. It's the wrong time of the year for them to be spawning in Gyminge Lake.

When she comes to the well-worn and much wider road between Blindhouse Wood and the border, she pauses. Hiding in the tall grasses to the side of her path, she takes a few moments rest . This is unknown territory. Although she cannot yet see it, she can hear the first stream just ahead. Her keen sense of smell has picked up the toad smell on the road that crosses her path. It is the main route between Gyminge Lake and the southern border worn smooth by thousands of toads over the centuries.

There'll be no need to ford the stream ahead; she'll just follow the road. Ahead of her as she turns south she spies, distant but in the same direction, a body of horsemen followed by a lonely horseman well to their rear. They are not Hardrada's men. These are uniformed soldiers. She wonders if they are goblins. She runs down along the inside of the hedges keeping them in view ahead. She dare not get too close and should not allow herself to be seen—yet.

THE TUNNEL

At Goblin Castle, the wizard has changed his mind about waiting for the return of his ambassador before blocking the tunnel. "Even though I would dearly like to hear news of the epidemic now raging through the farmhouse, it is a time of expected invasion of my country by the rebels. It will be wise to have my spy accepted by the invaders as even more than just a neutral. He should be considered a good friend. It will be better if Dr. Tyfuss remains on the other side of the border. I need to move quickly though. The Twith will be sure to be on their way without delay now that the weddings are over.

"I suppose it could happen that, by an unfortunate chance, the ambassador is with the invaders coming through the tunnel when it collapses to seal them in. Well, if so, in times of war one must expect casualties. It is impossible to come through conflict unscathed. It is like making an omelet. It requires the breaking of eggs. I must assume that the good doctor will be one of those eggs. Well, he can expect honor from his grateful country—a medal, a service of remembrance, and a memorial. There is a suitable spot near Fowlers Bridge that could benefit from a well designed statue. I will apply my mind to a suitably fitting tribute." He pulls himself back into the present. "It's not wise to get too far ahead of events."

Since the successful delivery of Gumpa's gift, the wizard has turned his attention to the trigger for the explosives he will use to block the tunnel. "I could do it myself, of course, by remote control. But in order for the timing to be just right, I would need to be on the spot. That will not be convenient when I need to be focusing on State affairs at Goblin Castle. I need some kind of detector in the tunnel itself. Perhaps I could use a trip wire. However, a toad or some other creature traveling through the tunnel could cause the explosion at the wrong time. The explosion needs to cause the maximum damage and trap all of the rebel Twith coming through the tunnel."

In the end he decides on a small radio device monitored by Major Bubblewick who replaced Colonel Tyfuss as Commander of the Southern Zone.

The wizard looks at the clock. "I need to be on my way. What would be the best way to travel? I'll be carrying a jar of very powerful liquid explosives as well as the trigger mechanism. Although it is faster to fly, that would be far too risky. I'll have to travel on horseback. I'll have the mail carrier be the rear escort—well to the rear—and he can carry the explosives in his saddlebag."

On this warm Sunday morning with scarcely any breeze, the wizard, with his escort of household cavalry, leaves Goblin Castle. Behind them, the lake glistens blue. It is a wonderful day for a ride in the country. The company heads up the hill to Blindhouse Wood. Occasionally the wizard breaks into song. A hundred paces behind them rides the daily mail courier—all by himself. He would have liked to have company alongside to chat with, but he is under strict orders to travel behind and alone.

At the fort on the southern border, all kinds of wild activity is in progress. Rasputin has brought warning of the wizard's arrival and put Major Bubblewick into a tizzy. All leave and off-duty time has been cancelled. Everything is being whitewashed, and there are new signs to everywhere unimportant. The kitchens are being rescrubbed and the menu for the day revised upwards.

On the wizard's arrival, he is immediately served tea and crumpets. He congratulates the major on the quality of his tea. "Where did you get such good blended tea? It definitely wasn't made with teabags. I don't allow them inside the castle gates. In fact, I'm inclined to ban their use throughout the kingdom. What do you think, major?"

"Oh, yes, sir. You are absolutely right. Only an infidel would use teabags! They definitely should be banned countrywide." The major has risen to his present rank by affirming everyone in authority above him. He is well practiced at it.

The wizard smiles with satisfaction. "I assume you have things well under control here."

"Yes. Of course, sir. Ever since the goblins were posted with lights in the tunnel, no toads have tried to come through. There is a toad constantly on watch at the waterfall end, but he hasn't caused any trouble. He is quite harmless and just watches what is going on."

"Very well. I have an assignment for you. I have information that the Twith from the Brook plan to invade our country. I intend to stop them. The tunnel will be blocked at both ends. After I set my device in place to block return to the entrance nearest the waterfall, your men will block this end.

"On the shelf in the center of the tunnel, I will place a lethal jar of liquid explosives and a small radio device, tuned to pick up noises. You will have a monitor to hear every sound. As soon as you hear Twith voices, you will reverse the switch to trigger the explosives. The five minute delay will be enough to let all the Twith filter forward into the trap. Once all the Twith have entered the tunnel, the explosives will detonate, bringing the roof of the tunnel crashing down behind them and locking them inside. It will bring an end forever to the nuisance of the free Twith." His laugh is sinister, but he thinks, *Such a pity about Dr. Tyfuss.*

The wizard turns to his raven. "Rasputin, I want you to go perch on a tree this side of the curtain where we waited for the exchange of the queen and the Book of Lore to take place. See whether the invaders and / or Dr. Tyfuss are yet on the way across the Brook."

As the bird lifts into the air and flies away from the camp, he fails to spot the slow movement of the tall grasses along the hedge as Loopy edges forward.

The dog can clearly see the entrance to a tunnel, and stealthily creeps towards it. There is a lot of activity going on, and she wants to take it all in and try to make some sense of it. She fixes into her mind, *A man on a black horse arrived and now appears to be in charge. He is dressed in all black and wears a black hat a size too small for him. I wonder if he can be the wizard that Bimbo talked about? He has the goblins bringing up stones to the tunnel entrance at the double.*

She hears him shout, "Bring those blocking stones closer, but keep them to the side out of sight. We don't want to alert the watching toad."

She sees the uniformed officer advance towards the tunnel. *He must be in charge of the goblins who were scurrying around earlier. He is carrying something very carefully in both hands and appears extremely nervous.*

After a while, Major Bubblewick, empty-handed and clearly happier, reappears at the mouth of the tunnel and hastens back to his office at the garrison camp.

Loopy now sees the man in black go down into the tunnel. She takes the opportunity to move closer to the tunnel mouth, but keeps well under cover. *I must be careful! I'm sure these people are active enemies of Bimbo and Scayper.* Now she can see down the long, straight tunnel until it disappears into the distance. It is well lit with lights at intervals.

The wizard does not want to alarm the watching toad until the very last minute. As he moves through the tunnel, he quietly tells each goblin, "Well done on keeping the tunnel lit. I want you to remain on duty until you hear a whistle blowing. When you do, gather your clutter and be ready to move! But not before you hear the whistle. Understood?" Each one answers respectfully, "Yes, sir," and straightens up just a bit more.

Griswold carefully sets his radio microphone in place on the shelf in the roof of the tunnel. He links wires from it to the jar of explosives the major so cautiously set there. He talks to the major. "Can you hear me?"

The answer comes back, "Loud and clear."

He lowers his voice. "How about now?"

"Yes, sir. I can still hear you."

He drops his voice to a whisper. "Can you still hear me?"

"Yes," comes the reply.

He sets the switches. Using dummy explosives at the castle, he checked that the mechanisms will trigger the explosion five minutes after the switch is reversed by Major Bubblewick. He sighs a heavy sigh. "It is unlikely that I will have the pleasure of throwing the switch myself. When you are a leader, you have to delegate your pleasures as well as your duties. Nevertheless, I'm enjoying setting things in place for the Big Bang." He is content that all is as it should be, and walks slowly back to the entrance.

Loopy sees him emerge with a swagger. There is a big, twisted smile on his face. The wizard whistles for Rasputin. "Everything is now in place. No need for you to watch any longer my good fellow."

Now Loopy hears the major blow his whistle. Goblins carrying lamps and haversacks begin emerging from the tunnel, walking fast. Darkness fills the tunnel as the last of them steps out.

Loopy listens carefully as the wizard immediately calls out orders to the goblins. "I want you to begin building a masonry wall. Place two pipes that are two arm spans in length on top of the first layer of stones so they extend halfway back into the tunnel. Later, near the center, there will be a spy-hole pipe with a wooden plug. And finally, a single pipe near the ceiling like the two lower ones."

The goblins work fast, and the wall is soon clearly visible from the far end where the toad is keeping watch. He dives into the waterfall pool to sound the alarm. It won't be long and all the toads on the Brook will be streaming towards the tunnel.

Loopy notices that there is no provision for a door in the wall. *I dare not wait any longer!* She charges for the tunnel and leaps between the goblins over the waist high wall into the unknown ahead. As she slows in the darkness to a cautious walk, she begins to hear distant splashing straight ahead.

The wizard is startled. "What kind of animal just raced past me?"

Rasputin isn't quite sure. "Boss, it looked like that wolf-dog from the farmhouse, but I can't explain how he ever got back into Gyminge."

Vyruss is just now climbing up the bank beside the waterfall. Tuwhit and Buffo brought him this far, and now he is caught up in a melee of toads rushing towards the tunnel.

Loopy doesn't notice the doctor as she dives over him into the pool below. Paddling to the surface, she squeezes past the toads coming through the falling water and heads towards the daylight beyond. As she hits the sunshine beyond the curtain, she enlarges!

This is something she wasn't expecting. As her brother had done almost three weeks earlier, she feels the shock of enlargement to Beyonder-size. The bog is carpeted with a mass of toads. Instead of the squelching of the bog, she experiences the squelching of toads. She gains her balance, wobbles unsteadily, shakes herself, and wonders, *Am I still who I was? I feel distinctly different!* She lets out a long, loud howl of surprise—a wolf howl.

It is good that Loopy traversed the tunnel before it is sealed shut, but for both the toads and Dr. Tyfuss, it is too late. In a few hectic moments of frantic activity, the tunnel has become wrapped in total darkness. The wall is complete to the roof and more stones are being piled hastily behind it to reinforce it.

The wizard smiles with satisfaction. He gives himself a mental pat on the back as he shares his joy with Rasputin. He can't keep the excitement out of his voice. "The curtain is closed so no pesky birds can get into Gyminge. The tunnel is closed to keep the rebel

Twith from invading my kingdom. All ways are sealed off. There is no way in. Gyminge is a fortress!" The wizard rubs his hands with glee. "Sort this one out, Rufus!"

LOOPY AT THE FARM

Gumpa and Lupus go off for their pre-afternoon tea walk to the pond without gran'ma. Although she would have liked the opportunity to share with her husband what lies behind the almost disastrous morning's events, she elected to stay behind with the children.

She talks things through with herself. She does that a lot. She has been told it is either a sign she is crazy or she has money in the bank. She prefers to think that the few funds she has in the bank are the reason. "Everyone has had a narrow escape from something, although I'm not quite sure what. Although calling the children to help the Twith at the beginning of the summer was well-intentioned, in hindsight perhaps it was not so wise. We seem to be almost helpless to prevent the wizard interfering at will with what goes on in the farmhouse or in the mansion below. One day one of his evil plots is sure to succeed. Clearly, it is certain that time is not on our side. Now that the weddings are over, we need to get on with the Return before something else bad happens.

"I wonder if, for the sake of the children's safety, we should consider calling off the whole enterprise and return the children to their parents? I know that the Twith will be devastated though. It would destroy any hope of their Return because one of the children is needed to lead the way." She tries to push the thought to the back of her mind. "I really need to discuss it with Gumpa. I wonder how much longer it will be before he gets back? Sometimes he wanders on down to Brook Lane and barely gets back in time for tea. We need to talk before then."

Her husband is not going to be long. Gumpa is at the bend in the road by the croc' pond tossing dried bread crusts to the mallard. The duck shows no inclination to come to the edge. It has come to distrust even the familiar.

Suddenly, without warning, Gumpa hears the unique, long, penetrating howl that Lupus aims every so often at the moon. He glances down at the animal beside him, but he is listening himself, ears stiffened straight upwards. He'd know that howl anywhere. He last heard that call centuries ago. It is as fresh as yesterday. He answers with his own delighted howl. "Welcome to the Brook sister."

Gumpa looks around in amazement and shakes his head to clear it. *Am I hearing double? Am I still suffering side effects from being doused in all that dust and powder this morning?*

Once he has howled, Lupus is off and running at top speed. Gumpa gasps in surprise. "What is he chasing? Where on earth is the dog going? For goodness sake, is he crazy? He's running straight onto the bog!"

He shouts loudly, "Lupus, what are you doing? Be careful!"

Gumpa knows there is a trail across the bog from the croc' pond to the waterfall that is capable of carrying a Beyonder. Both gran'ma and Mrs. Squidge walked it, and a dog's paw is distinctly smaller than a woman's foot.

Gumpa scoots as fast as he is able to the other side of the pond where he can see better. As he approaches the area closest to the waterfall, he hears strange sounds. "What is all that splashing? What's happening on the bog?"

The bog is alive with a host of swarming toads jumping and splashing. There are jumps and splashes all over the place. Most seem to be heading towards the waterfall lickety-split.

As soon as he can see across the bog towards the hidden waterfall, he stops in his tracks. It is not only his ears; it is also his eyes! He is seeing double! He blinks, rubs them, and looks again. It doesn't help. He tries rubbing them again, but there are still two identical wolf-dogs. He swallows hard, sits down, and places his head in his hands.

"What is happening? Ever since breakfast, this day has been filled with strange, unaccountable events. I need to get home, put a wet towel on my forehead and drink something strong like cough syrup or double-strength tea." He whistles to call Lupus. Not one, but two identical animals, ears proud and tails held high, begin running towards him. The leading dog has his head down, following a scented trail. The second dog merely follows and holds its head high.

When they arrive and nuzzle around his legs, he knows he is not imagining things. There is one dog to his left and another to his right. He reaches out. His left hand meets the cold nose of Lupus and the other the wagging head of his companion. He looks from one to the other then back again. He guesses from their behavior they are related or at least close friends. He tries to spot the differences. The head markings are a bit different, and the one on his right is slightly smaller. But the main difference is that one is a male and one a female.

Gumpa lifts his head and looks back at the massed toads on the bog. One of the jumpers is going against the flow, staying on the regular path and not splashing. It is Buffo coming towards him. On his back, the Ambassador of Gyminge to the Beyond is waving at him.

Gumpa is flabbergasted. "What a day this is proving to be! The strange events haven't stopped yet! Vyruss left on Tuwhit's back long before I left for my walk. What's he doing jumping around the bog on Buffo? He should be in Gyminge by now. I need to get back to the farmhouse. Maybe they'll know what's going on. There are signs that the wizard has struck again." Suddenly, he is anxious for gran'ma. He waits for Buffo to reach him, picks him up with the doctor still on his back, and hurries through the woods back up to the farmhouse.

The dogs race on ahead, tails streaming in an exuberance of happiness. They chase each other around the farmhouse. The only person who can initially make sense of what is happening outside is Elisheba. She knows them both. She hears the barking of two dogs, and picks up the differences of sound immediately. She looks out her upstairs window to verify what she already knows. She calls out to Taymar and to the couple next door. "Hooray! It's Loopy! She's come from Gyminge. Come quickly!" Grabbing her skirt around her, she flies downstairs towards Twith Mansion to the outside.

Sounds from the outside do not carry as easily into Twith Mansion. As she skitters through the living room, she yells the same message. The various rooms pour forth their occupants. Beginning at the entrance to the log and on up to the path on the bank, are eleven Little People and five Shadow children. They all watch with fascination as two wolf-dogs romp in the grass, chase and jump over each other, somersault, growl and snap at each other's tails.

Bingo is the only toad on the Brook that is not participating in the frantic activity on the bog. He is covering for his uncle as doorkeeper at Twith Mansion. Like the others around him, he wonders what is going on this crazy day.

Ambro and the two Shadow brothers, Bollin and Bimbo, have seen Loopy much more recently than Elisheba. They recognize her immediately. As they watch the dog and her brother rejoicing in her arrival, they wonder about Pru and Nettie. The two women were instrumental in helping them overcome Hardrada and his robber gang. Now Loopy will surely have some news of them. They hope it is not bad news.

The noisy barking and yelping brings the children pouring out of the sun porch door near the well. Forgotten for a while are the misadventures of the morning. They crowd into the yard to watch the dogs putting on a circus performance for their audience. Specs is curious. "How has Lupus somehow doubled himself?" Stormy fetches a chair for gran'ma to sit on.

Barney holds out his hand for any children who want to shrink. Several children take the opportunity. They immediately ask questions. Few of the Little People have explanations to offer. Jock tells them, "Time will make all thin's plain. Jus' enjoy!"

Gumpa comes into view walking briskly up the path from the Brook. He is puffing hard from the exertion. In his right hand is Buffo with the Ambassador of Gyminge to the Beyond on his back holding on tight with one hand to the toad's scaly skin. Gumpa turns the corner, and taking in the performance going on, allows himself a relieved smile. He slows to a halt at the sycamore tree, and lowers his hand to the ground permitting his two passengers to dismount. Quickly, he goes over to stand near his wife who looks at him with a question in her eyes. Gumpa just raises his eyebrows and shrugs his shoulders. Everything will have to wait until the two dogs decide to allow normal life to resume.

After a while, Gumpa whistles to Lupus. The dog slows, shakes his head, looks around to see where his new master is, and comes over to stand beside him. He barks sharply, twice. Loopy pauses her gymnastics, looks around for her brother, and joins him next to Gumpa. He wants an explanation of this new arrival and looks over towards Cydlo and Jock who are standing together. All conversation ceased when the barking stopped. Even the twittering of the birds has fallen to silence.

Bimbo starts filling in the picture for the others. He explains what he knows. "The new dog is Loopy. She belongs to Pru and Nettie, and is a full sister to Lupus. They sent her with us to show us the way when we went to rescue Bollin from Hardrada. We wouldn't have succeeded without her help. She returned home to Pru's cottage when we headed towards the waterfall and home. Welcome to Gibbins Brook Farm, Loopy! What are you doing here? Has something happened at the cottage? Are Pru and Nettie all right?"

LOOPY'S STORY

Loopy recognizes Bimbo's voice. Much sooner than she expected, her quest in the Beyond is over. "Pru told me to deliver the messages in my collar to either you, Bimbo, or to Scayper."

Gumpa sees that help is needed. The problem is that Loopy is no longer Gyminge-size but Beyonder-size. Neither of the two tiny people can reach her. He pats her head to reassure her, takes hold of her collar and unclips the collar pouch. He finds and carefully removes the two folded letters. "Shall I shrink them or shall I read them?"

None of them want to wait any longer. Bimbo tells his dad, "Just read it out to us."

Gumpa chooses Pru's letter first. He reads slowly, loudly and clearly. Apart from his voice there is complete silence.

Pru's Cottage, Gyminge

Dear Bimbo and Scayper,

> *Something odd happened just this morning. Both Nettie and I dreamed the same dream and it was about the pair of you, including a lot of your friends and a man wearing a woman's skirt. You were in terrible danger. We thought it was odd, but we think it is intended as a warning to you. Nettie is writing down the dream now and I am writing this covering letter to go along with it.*
>
> *We are sending Loopy with our letters. She seems confident she will be able to find you.*
>
> *We hope she will not have to go too far into the Beyond before she finds you. She has never been there before, but she is resourceful and will do her best.*

PLEASE be very, very careful if you are ever in a tunnel. Someone is trying to do you harm and the dream seemed as though he may have been successful.

When you no longer need Loopy, please send her back to us. We shall be missing her. Lovingly, Pru

Gumpa is thoughtful as he refolds the letter from Pru and opens Nettie's.

Pru's Cottage, Gyminge

Dear Scayper and Bimbo,

We have never had this happen before but, last night Pru and I had the same dream exactly! It was about both of you and a whole host of your friends. There must be some special meaning in this for we had not been talking about you yesterday at all.

In our dream both of you were dressed exactly as when we last saw you. You had many companions. There were men and women, boys and girls—more children than adults. Some of you were carrying weapons as though you were heading for a fight.

One among you, obviously a king, was a bearded, redheaded, older man wearing a crown and carrying a sword. Another, a young boy, was carrying a flag. Some were carrying lighted torches because it was dark all around you. The whole group was excited and happy, not at all frightened. Loopy was with you too.

There was the background sound of splashing water, but there was no water to be seen. You were passing through a large, dark, dry tunnel when suddenly there was the sound of an explosion behind you. It was followed by the heavy rumble of falling rock, and then complete darkness.

I woke up and rubbed my eyes wondering if the roof of the cottage had fallen in.

Neither Pru nor I were in the dream itself. Please be very careful if you ever go into a tunnel with your friends.

Nettie

Bimbo asks his father, "Do you think Loopy will be going back soon? If that is so, you need to write a reply for her to take back to Pru and Nettie."

Gumpa shakes his head, and raises his hand to ask for silence. "Listen, everyone! Here is some more fresh news. It looks as though Loopy only just got through the tunnel in time. Buffo brought Vyruss back because there is no longer any way through the tunnel. The wizard has blocked the tunnel at the Gyminge end with a wall. The toads are having a meeting at the waterfall right now to work out what, if anything, they can do. It looks as though there is no way for Loopy to get back home at present. Nor is there a way for us into Gyminge.

"Before we settle down to have Loopy tell us what she saw and heard as she was leaving Gyminge, and consider the letters we just heard, let's make sure the farmhouse is secure against any secret intruder trying to gain entry while we are all out here. Austin and Lucas, will you go check that all the windows and doors in the house are securely latched? You can leave this near porch door unlocked."

He looks up to the chimney slab and sees Tuwhit swinging in to join Crusty. The owl took Buffo and Bingo over to the waterfall and is just returning minus his passengers. Gumpa nods with approval. "Good. The guards and precautions are all in place to keep the farm safe."

It looks like tea is going to have to wait this afternoon, so gran'ma asks Rachael, "Will you go check that I turned off the stove and the lights? I think the only one I might have left on is the one in the kitchen, but maybe you better check all of them. Thanks."

As the children return from their errands, Gumpa says, "You will want to hear what Loopy has to say, so you better shake hands with one of the Twith." The children have become accustomed to Lupus and understand what his various whines, sniffles, grunts and barks mean without actually understanding what he says. But Loopy doesn't know how to communicate that way. It will be much easier if her listeners are small and can understand what she is saying.

Gumpa speaks to Loopy. He doesn't have to be Twith-size to talk to the animals. "If you can tell us what is happening in Gyminge, it will help us to better consider what we might do. Please tell us everything you saw and heard at the Gyminge end of the tunnel."

Lupus barks instructions to his sister to tell them slowly what she saw as she approached the tunnel on the Gyminge side and what happened. "Don't omit any detail. Everything you saw is important if we are ever going to get back home."

Loopy explains, "After I left the cottage, I ran along the edge of Blindhouse Wood eastwards. I was looking for a river that might run south to the border into the Beyond. I smelled water ahead. Although I couldn't understand why, I also smelled a strange, strong toad smell. A well-worn path headed south. I heard the sound of flowing water beyond, and decided to follow the trail. Traveling in the same direction just ahead of me was a group of horsemen. They were mostly uniformed goblins. A single horseman followed well to their rear. I kept out of sight, running along the inside of the hedges a good distance back. Far ahead was a line of trees that I discovered marked the border.

"When the horsemen arrived, there was great activity from the hundreds of men already there. Men were running everywhere. The goblins saluted the man dressed in black who was riding a big black horse. I could see the dark opening marking the entrance to the tunnel. Stealthily, I crept as near as I dared. Goblins were bringing up big building stones at the double. The man in black ordered the stones to be brought closer to the tunnel, but he wanted them kept out of sight to avoid alerting the toad at the other end.

"He sent a raven off to keep watch at the other end of the tunnel. I noticed the bird had a broken beak. Then the uniformed officer in charge of the scurrying goblins disappeared into the tunnel. He was carrying something very carefully in both hands. It looked like a jar of pickles, but he was very nervous and walked slowly with his head down to be sure he didn't trip. A short while later he reemerged, empty-handed. He look relieved and hastened to a tent near the entrance. Then the man in black entered the tunnel.

"While he was inside the tunnel, I worked my way closer to the tunnel mouth keeping well under cover. It was a long, straight tunnel lit with lights at intervals. I could see down the full length of the tunnel until it disappeared in the distance.

"Several minutes later, the man in black came back. He called for his raven. They stayed close to the entrance ready to organize the wall building.

"A whistle sounded and goblins carrying lamps began pouring out of the tunnel, walking fast. The tunnel was now total darkness. Just inside the mouth of the tunnel, other goblins began to build a masonry wall. There was no space for a door in the wall, but they laid pipes that extended into the tunnel across the first layer of stones."

Vyruss raises his hand. He has been listening carefully, thinking hard. His mind is going like the clappers and he has a question. He thinks he knows the answer, but wants to be sure. "When the goblins were building the wall, were they just putting blocks on top of each other, or were they setting them in lime mortar the way walls are usually built?"

Loopy is quite certain. "Oh, there was no time for that, although I suppose they could have used mortar on the back face of the wall after it was raised. No, the stones that had prepared faces squared off were in a special pile. It looked like they were being used dry on the inside face of the wall with the rougher stones behind them.

"I didn't dare wait any longer. The way to the Beyond would soon be closed. I had to take a giant leap between the goblins to get over the waist high wall into the darkness. I couldn't see anything in the tunnel, but I soon heard distant splashing straight ahead. I hoped it was the waterfall Bimbo talked about.

"It was, and I dived through the falling water towards the daylight beyond. As I went through the curtain I grew into a giant dog! My skin felt as though it had stretched fit to burst! *wow!* I was caught by surprise and let out a long, loud howl. I heard an answering howl and knew, without understanding how it could be, that it was my brother. The rest you know."

DEALING WITH ROBBERS

Back in Goblin Castle, the wizard is busy. His mind is focused. Mottoes float through his thoughts in profusion. *A true leader never rests. Be alert at all times!* He congratulates himself. "My people can hardly realize how fortunate they are to have a leader like myself. Where will they ever find another so full of energy and never at rest? One with a wide-ranging mind so committed to their welfare? A leader fights enemies both at home and abroad. The enemies yapping at the border are not the only ones to deal with. There are enemies at home waiting for an opportunity to link up in an alliance with those abroad. Their mottoes are *'Unite and conquer'*. That is not my way. Allies are unreliable and untrustworthy. My mottoes are *'Rely on yourself, not on others'*. *'Divide and conquer'*.

"My successful journey to the Brook to deliver the gift for Gumpa was a complete success. By now the overseas enemies have opened their package of trouble and are still trying to cope with it. I can expect a long lull in events until the ambassador comes back to report. However, the blockage of the tunnel is going to prevent that until I open it up again.

"Now it is time to deal with the enemies within. I have invited King Haymun for tea and to have a game of chess to keep our minds active. I wonder whether I should allow the king to win? After all, I have beaten him in all thirty-seven games we have played so far. No, I can't do that. My brain and pride won't allow it."

King Haymun arrives promptly at three. The opponents face each other across the table. Each player is waiting for the attention of the other to be distracted from the board in order, unseen, to move a piece to his own advantage. As they play, they discuss King Haymun's recent misadventure. A little over a fortnight ago, while the wizard was dealing with urgent matters on the Brook, the king was kidnapped from his own bedroom in the castle. Three escapees from the castle dungeons seized him at sword point and took him north. Later that same day, he reappeared alone and on foot at the fort on the southern border. His story of battling his way to freedom by immense and continuous acts of courage carries little weight with the wizard. Each time the king tells it, the story becomes enlarged and gets more and more embellished.

Griswold is in a mellow mood and turns earnestly to the king. Although he is winning easily, his razor-sharp brain memorizes where all of the remaining pieces are placed in case the king has any ideas of moving a piece while they are talking."Haymun, I want you to go over again the details of what happened at the robber camp. This is the kind of enemy we can expect to be disloyal to our country in any time of national emergency. We don't want to be fighting on two fronts. We shall deal with them one by one. I am planning an expedition against the camp that I might ask you to lead. However, I will probably accompany you. We don't want a long, drawn-out engagement with a lot of blood spilled. Just a sharp and decisive punitive expedition."

The king quickly removes his hand away from the board as though it has been scalded. He feels the cold, clammy hand of fear creeping up and down his spine. Even the last remark is not comforting. It could be his blood that gets spilled!

The wizard continues. "In order to help with the planning, go through again everything that happened to you there. Describe the location of the camp and its layout, everything that you can think of that might help in planning an attack."

The king desperately searches his mind. *I need to remember, and remember correctly, the stories I previously told the wizard. I must keep away from what happened to me and concentrate on the description of the gang and their camp. That is what the wizard is really after, and it is less likely to get me into trouble.*

208

He speaks confidently. "The camp is in Blindhouse Wood, in an open clearing almost at its western edge. It is a large clearing. A stream runs along the west edge of it so it is a good location for their camp. The stream provides water for the robber gang and is enough to serve all their purposes. They feel they are absolutely safe and do not post guards. They are about twenty strong and have a wicked reputation. Many seem to have wives and children.

"Hardrada is the robber chief. He is a giant of a man with long, shaggy, black hair hanging loose, bearded, and strong as an ox. The man could crush stones to dust between two of his fingers. The others all seem to be frightened of him.

"Hardrada is the only one who lives in a tree house. There is a great oak on the northwest edge of the clearing and the limbs have conveniently spread out in all four directions at about the same height. These limbs support the floor and then the walls and roof of the house. A little more than a man's height above the ground, reached by a portable ladder, is the wooden platform that forms both the outside porch and the floor for the dwelling. Sometimes people swing onto his house platform using ropes. There are several hanging ropes suspended from the extended limbs of the oak above and one from a neighboring sycamore. He uses them himself to get to the ground.

"The men live in huts around the edge of the clearing. There is a stable on its south side at the edge of the stream. Next to the stable they have a special hut where they keep their prisoners. The walls are solid oak. That is where they kept me. They have no need for guards on the prisoners. The area all around the prisoner's hut is fenced. Outside the door is the biggest dog I have ever seen kept half starved.

"The inside of Hardrada's house is one large room, as large as the spread of the supporting oak limbs will permit. There are windows towards the clearing and towards the sunset. There are no windows towards the stable or, on the opposite side, to the north. Various robber wives provide Hardrada with food when he is not eating with his men."

The wizard looks at the time. He is thinking carefully. "Haymun, my friend, do you think you could find your way back to the camp?"

If there is one thing that Haymun never wants to do, it is to find his way back to Hardrada's camp again. Or even ever be anywhere closer than a mile to where the man might be. The mere thought of the man terrifies him. He tries to remember whether he ever told the wizard he was blindfolded. He is unsure about that, and dares not make a mistake.

"If you follow the southern flank of the forest you would come to the stream that runs past their camp. I would think that perhaps Rasputin could find it without too much trouble."

"Yes, that is a good idea. Rasputin and I will go take a quick check. You have given me a good idea of what to look for. If I fail to find it, I will come back and get you. We need to move on this quickly because things are heating up at the tunnel also. Leave the rest of your story for the time being. And, oh, leave the game where it is. We'll finish it later.

"While we are away, I want you to organize a company of one hundred of our best cavalry. They are to be ready to move at first light tomorrow under your command. They must be prepared to move quickly. Ensure they are fully armed and have spare horses. There may be hard fighting. We will teach those rascals a lesson. Take field rations for three days. If we need more, we'll get supplies from Major Bubblewick."

King Haymun goes white in the face. His mind whirls frantically. *I wonder whether a sudden attack of appendicitis could help me? I'm afraid though, that in the absence of Dr. Tyfuss, the wizard might choose to operate himself.* He tries to muster enthusiasm for the prospect of the attack on the camp, but that is a lie too hard even for him to swallow. He manages to force out a few words without trembling. "I wish you well and may you find success in your journey. Now, if you will excuse me, sir. I need to get my men organized." He hurries out the door wiping the sweat from his brow with his sleeve.

As soon as he leaves, the wizard moves one of his own pawns one square ahead. He snickers. "That will nicely block the developing attack on my bishop."

As he goes out to talk to Rasputin, he wonders, *What shall I be? A raven or a cormorant or a duck? It's possible the robbers might feel duck soup will be a welcome change of diet. A raven will be safest. While I'm about it, I may as well put a bubble over the robbers' camp. That will stop them causing any trouble in the neighborhood as my troops surround the camp tomorrow.* He chuckles with delight at his genius.

The wizard and the raven have no difficulty finding the robber camp. King Haymun gave good directions. Griswold flies in a circle around the entire area that he wishes to enclose with his secret weapon. As he does so, he reflects, "It's a mere matter of using the unique skills I possess. By uttering a few special words chosen and designed by myself, a strong, impenetrable curtain is at once in place. It will soon begin closing itself at the top to form a bubble, and those inside will not be able to threaten our advance in any way. Any arrows they fire or spears they throw will only bounce off the inside of the bubble and be flung right back at them. I won't make it very high—I don't need to—only tall enough to cover the oak tree."

He smiles with satisfaction. "I first perfected the bubble while I was the chief librarian at King Druthan's castle in Cornwall. I put one over the prize cherry tree in the king's garden. Unfortunately, it led to my banishment. When I invaded Wozzle, I just used the curtain and didn't cover it over. But I used bubbles successfully to conquer Gyminge. Taymar's brother, Ambro, found himself trapped inside one of those. The seven rebel Twith managed to escape before I completed the even stronger curtain that now surrounds my entire kingdom."

Rasputin is impressed. "Wow, boss. That didn't take you any time at all. Boy! Are they ever going to be surprised when any of them try to venture outside their camp!"

The wizard grins with appreciation. He is pleased with his performance. "Right, my good lad. Let's be on our way back to the castle for a short night's rest."

THE ROBBER CAMP

The wizard rouses King Haymun at far too early an hour to suit the king's need for a full night's sleep. "Sound reveille and get your troops ready to move out. Each man is to take with him a coil of new rope. There's no need for you to take the longer journey to the south of Blindhouse Wood. Since I located the robber camp and erected a bubble around it, you can safely take the most direct route straight through Blindhouse Wood. I will join you before mid-morning and guide you the last portion of the way."

It is the same route, in the reverse direction, that Queen Sheba rode when she was released to the wizard by her robber captors centuries ago. The wizard has always resented the amount of ransom he was forced to pay Hardrada for the queen he was holding hostage. Griswold has nursed a giant-sized grudge all these years. Recently, the man ignited the wizard's wrath by seeking to do the same with King Haymun! The wizard was thrown into turmoil and shouted at the castle walls, "He is willing to take on the whole government and hold it to ransom! If it hadn't been for the monarch's courage in escaping during a session of torture, I would have been the victim of the robber's extortion once again. This time there is going to be a settling of accounts. Getting revenge is the only right way to put a grudge to rest."

Griswold is in a good mood as he sees off King Haymun and his hundred cavalrymen. "I'm surprised to see the king riding in the middle of his troops. Why on earth is he doing that? I'll reprimand him about it when I see him. They are making good time, though."

King Haymun is not in nearly as good a mood as the wizard. He mutters unhappily to himself, "The wizard is confident that he has all the robbers penned up. I'm not so sure. Suppose they still had raiding parties out on the rampage as the bubble was positioned? I'm staying in the middle of my troops. It's safer than being either out in front or back at the rear."

In fact, the wizard did not completely enclose all of the robber compound. In order to have some intermediary to work through, Griswold did not include the lone rough hut on the very edge of the clearing that is somewhat isolated from the other dwellings. From the scattered clutter around it, it appears that a family with a number of children live there. That alone has been excluded from the bubble.

As the goblin cavalry gallops through Blindhouse Wood, they pass close to the cottage inhabited by Pru and Nettie. The women can hear the sounds of hoofs, the jingle of harness, the snatches of song, and the occasional shouted command. It is clear the horsemen are heading towards Hardrada's camp. There is no attempt at quiet or secrecy. Pru wonders, *What is going on? I wish Loopy were here. She could go find out for us.*

By this time, two ravens are ahead of the cavalry column. The wizard shouts to Rasputin. "You guide them on in from here. I'm going ahead to see what's happening at the compound." He perches on a lower branch of the nearby sycamore tree. If he could laugh, he would. "Just look at all the confusion I've caused in the robber camp! If they're surprised now, they are going to be a lot more surprised shortly."

Scarface and his family are the ones who ended up outside the bubble. They cannot understand what happened. Their companions are trying to get out; they are trying to get in. Eventually, by trying to touch hands with those inside, Scarface figures out that there is something flexible between them. They cannot see it, but they can feel it. Whatever it is, it prevents anyone from passing through it.

Mrs. Scarface wants to hang out her washing. Unknown to her, the clothesline is on the other side of the barrier. When she approaches near, the unseen obstruction tosses her clothes basket out of her hand. Now all her clean laundry is lying in the mud.

Their twelve unruly children, also dirty, want to go play with their friends now that breakfast is over. All twelve are crying and whimpering because they cannot do so.

Scarface tries cutting the unseen skin with both his dagger and his sword, but they are too blunt to make any impression.

Those inside try the same tactics without success. Several try digging down below the barrier, but that doesn't do any good either.

Hardrada has just come out the door of his tree house. The wizard has never met him, although he knows his reputation. There is no difficulty identifying him from King Haymun's description. He is a truly huge man with a wild mop of black hair both on his head and around his face.

Grabbing onto one of the ropes, Hardrada launches off the porch for a quick descent to the ground. He is not aware of the obstruction between him and the neighboring tree. How could he be? He cannot see it! *BOINGG!* He bounces to and fro wondering what hit him and keeps on hitting him. Releasing his grasp, he crashes to the ground and tumbles in a heap.

His men and their families quickly gather around him. They are near panic-stricken. The late arrival of their leader seems to unsettle the robbers even further. "We're accustomed to taking off into the deep woods in the early morning. We cannot do so. We get so far and...*BOINGG!* We are forced back. What's happened? We've sent our children and dogs searching for any escape opening. They can't find one. They just keep going *BOINGG!*"

They want answers. The questions fly fast and furious. "What are we to do?" "Who has done this?" "How did they do it?" "What is going to happen now?"

Hardrada himself is asking questions of his lieutenants. "Has everything possible been checked? What about directly above? Can someone climb the longest rope and get out that way?"

One of the bowmen fires an arrow upwards. It flies higher than the surrounding trees. *BOINGG!* It drops back down and the bowman jumps to one side. The arrow didn't even stick to whatever the roof is made of.

This is clearly an emergency for the entire robber camp. Hardrada shouts, "This may take some time to figure out. Every man bring something to sit on." There is a mad scramble as chairs are dragged from the dwellings. They form a large, rough circle. The men sit, and the wives, together with their children that can be corralled, sit on the ground at the feet of their husbands.

As they discuss the situation, there are plenty of questions, but no answers. No one knows what and when this happened. They have no idea about what they can do. The fear is that if nothing can be done, then they are doomed to slowly starving to death. Most of the vegetable gardens are beyond the perimeter of the unseen barrier. Scarface and his family are going to have plenty to eat, but the rest of them are not so fortunate. They have always taken their water needs from the stream, and now that is no longer accessible. They consider trying to dig out the well they filled in because it was a danger to the toddlers.

The raven watching them takes off. He has heard enough, and he has also heard the sound of approaching horses. He flies up the path and lands in front of them. In a split instant he resumes his full stature and appearance as the Wizard of Wozzle. The column comes to a halt. and he mounts one of the spare horses. Rasputin, his present task as guide completed, flies higher and perches in the nearest oak tree where he has a good view of what is going on below.

The wizard beckons King Haymun forward and they ride to the front of the column. The leading cavalrymen straighten their hanging pennants, the others hold their lances vertical. The wizard gives them their orders. "You are to completely surround the camp. Once you have done that, face in towards the center of the clearing and lower your lances. Then edge forward until you feel the unseen bubble skin resist your forward movement. When you do, stop and raise your lances to the vertical. Remain stationary and wait for further orders."

The cavalry bugler is that unreliable boy who never plays the right tune. He has increased his repertoire by hard practice. He practices constantly and drives his neighbors in the barracks to request compassionate transfers. Although the boy is good at the tunes he knows, he doesn't know what tune is going to emerge from his bugle until he sounds off the first note. Whatever lead note happens to emerge determines which tune will follow. In this case, it is *Three Blind Mice*.

As the weird bugle call peels out along the forest path and into the robber clearing, the horsemen move forward. The wizard and King Haymun halt as they reach the edge of the clearing. The two files behind them separate to the left and right, and form up in a circle around the bubble. Lances are lowered, and the horses jostle and shuffle themselves forward. One by one the lances are raised vertical and the hanging pennants drape along the lance shafts.

A space has been left between the horsemen for the wizard and the king. They ride forward and rein to a halt. Scarface, who has scuttled back in fear to the safety of his own doorway, is beckoned forward. His wife pushes him out the door, fearful for the brood of children hanging onto her skirts. His oldest daughter grabs her father's hand and runs alongside him. He is glad she is there.

"What is your name, man?"

He responds nervously, fearing for his life. "People call me Scarface, sir. It is not my real name. My real name is…"

"Enough, man. Now listen, Scarface. I am going to send you inside. Do as I tell you and you will be all right. First tell them that any man who moves other than yourself risks his life. Then give them this message. I, the Wizard of Wozzle, am the government and I am after Hardrada. It is only Hardrada I want. At this time

I shall be satisfied with him, but I want Hardrada and I am going to have him! I may take any captives you have in your jail as well. For the rest of you, I will leave you your horses, but you must surrender all your weapons. I also want assurance that you will return to lawful behavior and limit yourselves to lawful pursuits in the future. As you can see, my men are completely surrounding you. If you fail to give me the assurance I ask, then I will order my men to lower their lances and move forward.

"Scarface, the choice is theirs. Go and tell them they have fifteen minutes to decide. If you are not back with their reply by then, we will charge ahead and destroy everything in our path. I am an impatient man, and no less ruthless than your own leader. Be on your way. Walk straight ahead. I have already opened the way in for you."

DECISION AMONG THIEVES

Scarface is scared stiff. He is scared stiff of the man on the horse behind him and he is scared stiff of the man he is about to face. He walks forward slowly, his heart and mind in turmoil. *I wish that any other than myself had been chosen to be the messenger. I could never remember poetry verses at school. Right now, my mind is teetering on the edge of a vacuum and about to fall in.* He glances down at his daughter walking into the bubble beside him. *I hope Rowena will be able to help me. I don't mind admitting that she is brighter than I am or ever was. Gets it from her mother. She could probably repeat word for word what she just heard.* He asks her, "Do you remember everything he said?"

The girl nods, her eyes large with excitement.

He breathes a sigh of relief, and steps out more confidently. He stops in front of Hardrada. Those gathered around their chief are shouting at him from all directions. "Speak up so that we can all hear, Scarface!" "What does he want?"

Hardrada himself says nothing.

The scarred little man speaks up at the top of his voice. Amazingly his mind has kicked into overdrive and he recalls the wizard's words with near perfection. "He says he, the Wizard of Wozzle, is the government. He says that any man who blinks an eyelid, other than me, he'll have his life. He is after Hardrada and he wants Hardrada. That's why he has come. He is the only one he is after right now, but he says he may take our prisoners. That would be Skweejee because we don't have any other prisoners. All the rest of us must promise to behave ourselves in the future. From this moment on, we have to stop the way we have been living and become law-abiding citizens. If we do that, he will leave us alone."

A lone voice calls out, "And what happens if we don't give up Hardrada and we like the way we live and aren't going to change it?"

Rowena turns to the man and answers with a voice that is loud and shrill. "If you fail to do what he says, he will remove the thing that he put around us, and tell his men to chop us all into little bits! He says that the choice is yours, and you have fifteen minutes to decide. If you agree, he will let you keep your horses, but you have to give up all your weapons. Dad has to tell him what we decide before time runs out. The man said that he eats snakes for breakfast and isn't used to waiting."

The same voice shouts, "Go back, Scarface, and ask him what he's going to do with Hardrada. We're all in this together."

Scarface and Rowena scurry off to find out.

Hardrada has remained silent, but his scowl is nervous and uncertain. He looks around at his men. He isn't sure what to think. *We have been together for years, through thick and thin together, but is there anyone I can really rely on? A few of us might escape in the melee of a fight, but will I be one of them? How can we fight anyway when we can't get our hands on the enemy? Many of the gang are my close friends. They have wives and children, and they are sure to be the first to get hurt in any fighting. They are kind of my family too. I don't really want them to get knocked about.*

The wives are letting their husbands know what they think. The husbands already know what they themselves think. *The jig is up! We have had a good run and there have been many rich pickings over the years, but it's game over now. We are fortunate he only wants Hardrada. He could easily take all of us and mete out the same treatment as Hardrada is likely to get. It's too bad about Hardrada, he's been a leader we could rely on to lead from the front, but, well, the jig is up for him too. It's just a question of playing out the game at the dictates of the man outside. The goblin cavalry surrounding us has the upper hand. They will decide all the moves. We could protest as much as possible, but compliance is inevitable.* Without admitting it to each other, they are working out their own ways of meeting the wizard's condition of becoming law-abiding citizens. They will need to take their families and disappear into the countryside. Some are wondering whether there are any vacancies in the goblin army. Others question the kind of reception they will get when they go back home.

Scarface and Rowena are back. "He says that Hardrada will get the justice he deserves. There are many gallons of blood on his hands, and he will be taken to Goblin Castle and put in the dungeon until he is tried for his crimes. He will have an opportunity then to put forward his defense. He also says there are only four minutes left and he is in a hurry. What do we want to do?"

Hardrada rises to his feet and holds his hands out wide. He is still, for a few moments more, the leader. There is complete silence. He speaks loudly and calmly. "I never thought it would come to this, but you men do not need to decide. I have already decided. We will accept the conditions we have been given. We are overwhelmed and we have no choice but to submit. I surrender to the force around us. If you also agree to the terms affecting you, raise your right fists."

It is a ragged response that spreads over a long minute. No one wants to show willingness to abandon their leader to his fate, but a majority of arms are lifted. Hardrada looks around and nods his head to those needing encouragement to join in the surrender of the freedom that has been so important to them. Soon all the men have their right arms lifted high.

A sharp order from the robber chief is directed at Scarface. "Take our reply back to the wizard. We accept all of his demands."

Once again, Scarface and Rowena scurry off towards the wizard.

Hardrada continues. "Men, do not remain here in this camp for you will receive abuse and blame from those who live around you. As you disperse, take with you my good wishes. Take care of your children, and nourish the good memories they will have of your time here. Perhaps we shall meet again, but most likely we shall not. If I leave any debts among you, I ask your forgiveness. Share among yourselves any of my possessions that remain. Stay seated to wait and do as the goblins say. Now I say goodbye to you, and thank you for your help over the years." He sits back down and puts his head in his hands.

The mounted magician and the king have heard what has been said, and have seen the raised arms of submission, but they wait impassively until Scarface and his daughter arrive.

The smile on Scarface's face almost prevents him from delivering the message with a sense of solemnity. "The terms you demanded for Hardrada and his men have been accepted. What must we do now?"

The wizard nods his acceptance of the surrender. "Take these two coils of rope and bind Hardrada so that he cannot move. Bind his hands firmly behind his back, and bind his feet together. Use his head scarf to blindfold him. Bring his horse and have two men hold it still. You and five others lay your chief across the saddle. We shall check carefully what you have done, so don't try any tricks or I shall leave all of you confined as you are. And tell those noisy children to stop crying!"

Scarface yells at the children on his way back. "He says to shut up the kids crying. He can't stand the noise."

Rowena carries one of the coils of rope and Scarface the other. He informs Hardrada of the wizard's instructions. The big man, without a word, rises to his feet and walks slowly to the center of the circle of chairs. He puts his feet together, places his hands behind his back, and waits. Scarface picks five men near Hardrada to truss their leader and makes his way over to the stable.

Skweejee stands in the doorway. He is a goblin captive and lives in the stable among the horses. He dares to hope that this is going to be his lucky day and he will be free once again. Not quite three weeks ago, he experienced temporary freedom as Bimbo and Scayper freed him and Bollin. Although he was fast asleep, they bundled him on a horse and took him with them. Unfortunately, it was not far enough. He woke up in a meadow with his horse tethered to a nearby tree. He was jolted awake by a kick from a robber boot, and it was a case of back to the grind once again without ever really enjoying his liberty.

Skweejee and Scarface, working together, saddle and harness Hardrada's horse. Skweejee wonders about a horse for himself. There are spare horses in the stable. He makes a quick decision. It may be now or never. He saddles and prepares another for himself and leads this to the stable door where he mounts it. Taking the reins of Hardrada's horse, he leads the animal to the center of the clearing. He remains, mounted and motionless, while the trussed and blindfolded leader of the gang is lifted and balanced across the saddle of the larger black horse, the biggest in the stable.

King Haymun recognizes Skweejee from his previous visit and draws in a hiss of breath. Frantic thoughts race across his mind. *What does the groomsman remember of what really happened that day? If he blabs his mouth off, I might really be in hot water! Not only hot water, in superheated steam!*

Skweejee leads Hardrada's horse through the bubble and halts alongside King Haymun. Haymun noisily calls forward two of the cavalrymen to check that the ropes binding Hardrada are secure. They also rope the robber leader to the horse so that he will not slip or slide off. While the wizard is turned away, issuing his final orders to Scarface, the king whispers anxiously, "Say nothing, nothing at all. okay?"

Skweejee knows desperation when he sees it, and nods. He is in the goblin army where promotions and punishments are in the king's domain most of the time. He knows which side his bread is buttered on, and nods again.

The king has a quiet conversation with the wizard. He also nods in agreement, but to a different question. Haymun turns to the stable boy. "We are sending Hardrada on ahead. His bonds are secure so there can be no wriggling loose. You and fifty of the cavalry are to return to the castle immediately. You shall continue to lead Hardrada's horse by the reins, but you and he will be in the middle of the group. You will, of course, be traveling much more slowly than the later party. However, if you do arrive before I do, the cavalry sergeant major is to personally oversee that the blindfolded Hardrada is placed in the most secure of the dungeon cells. He is to be manacled and placed in leg irons before being fed a meal. Is that all clear?"

Skweejee is not the brightest groomsman in the stable, but this is a fairly easy and straightforward assignment. He says confidently, "Yes, your majesty."

After the shouted orders to move out have receded into the distance, it is time to collect the weapons. The wizard gives Scarface some lengthy instructions. "Take this message to your friends inside the bubble and hurry back. Tell them they are to return to their homes. Then, they are to bring out every weapon in the house and stack them in a pile on the north side of the compound. They are to bring not only their swords, daggers, bows and arrows, but even the smallest of weapons—peashooters, catapults, slings and anything that can be described as a weapon. That includes all the children's toys as well. When every home, including Hardrada's own, has been emptied, they are to gather on the south side of the clearing while the homes on the north side are searched and checked. Any home where a weapon is found will be set alight."

Scarface delivers his message and returns, dragging a reluctant Rowena with him. She wanted to stay with her friends. He gives a rough salute, and announces, "Sir, the men have all been told to heap their weapons on the north side of the clearing. All the men and their families, other than my own family, will stand on the south side when they are finished. I don't want my own house burned down, so I will stack all my weapons, and any belonging to the children, outside my door." He runs to do so.

The wizard closes the bubble off behind them. It is time for a tea break. The cavalry are also given time for refreshments. The wizard and the king lean their backs against the bubble and allow themselves the glow of having brilliantly commanded a military operation safely executed and concluded.

Now Griswold gives orders to his troops. "Men, I'm going to shrink the bubble southwards so that it no longer covers the houses or the piled weapons on the north side. When I do, move forward. Those of you on the east select any of the weapons that can be of use to the cavalry back at the castle. The rest are to be trampled on by the horses until they are ground into dust or broken beyond repair. Those of you on the west, search the houses for any other weapons. If you find anything, set the house on fire. When you have finished, return to your former positions."

Once the north side has been checked, the wizard expands the curtain to cover the north side. He orders Scarface, "Go stand at the small opening I left and shout to your friends to gather on the north side, and then step back quickly before I close the opening."

The robbers within the bubble have no chance to break and run for cover in the woods as they move across the clearing. Once they are all on the north side, the wizard moves the curtain back to uncover the stable, the prisoner's hut and the other dwellings. Now the wizard's men on that side investigate every home. They find nothing remotely resembling a weapon. Everything has been cleared out. All the robbers know that with even one small hut ablaze, there will be no containing the inferno that will sweep right through the camp.

The wizard gives Scarface a choice. "Do you and your family want to remain outside of the bubble, or do you wish to join the others inside?"

He chooses freedom. "If you please, sir, we will remain outside."

KENNETH G. OLD & PATTY OLD WEST

"Very well. I have one last message for you to deliver. To prevent any attempt at pursuit and the rescue of your leader, the bubble will remain closed until my troops have returned to the castle. As soon as my men are back at the castle, I will remove the bubble so your friends and their families will be free to go where they wish. That should be no later than noon. I trust they will not be overly hungry or thirsty by then.

"One last warning. If any adverse report about this camp reaches me, I will permanently seal it off so that no one shall ever again be able to enter it or leave it. And I can do it without leaving my castle. Is that understood?"

It is. As soon as Scarface is back outside the bubble for the last time, the bubble is sealed tight and the cavalry forms up for the gallop back to Goblin Castle.

The wizard is pleased with himself. He mentally pats himself on the back. *Such superb planning, Griswold. It has been a good morning's work! I'll fly back with Rasputin and check on the advance party along the way. There are preparations to be made in the dungeons for the visitor. Then after lunch, it will be time to relax, and perhaps enjoy a bowl of cherries, or maybe even two, while the king and I finish our chess game.* He breaks into song. "Tra-la-la-la. Life couldn't be better!"

THE TUNNEL CLOSURE

Over on the Brook, afternoon tea is underway. The refreshing rhythm of teatime is an old English household tradition. It rejuvenates body and soul until dinner time. After tea, Gumpa and gran'ma will join the Twith downstairs in Twith Mansion to discuss the day's events and what, if any, plans are possible. Cydlo has said that any of the children who wish to join in the discussion are welcome to come. He especially wants Specs to be present. He has grown to admire and respect the boy's wisdom and common sense.

Two dogs rather than one now share the carpet in front of the hearth. Gumpa is drinking his third cup of tea and has his slippered feet on the back of Lupus as usual. Gran'ma sits opposite Gumpa in her own wing-backed chair. She is not all that keen on dogs but allows Loopy to lay quite close to her feet. She is more relaxed now that the weddings are over and she can concentrate on the normal routine of having sixteen houseguests. They are usually full-sized, but more and more they enjoy shrinking to Twith-size to spend time downstairs in Twith Mansion.

Gumpa is thoughtful. He decides to ask gran'ma's opinion. "Loopy promised to share early news of Gyminge and her adventures living with Pru and Nettie. She plans to start long, long ago when Elisheba first visited the cottage. I wonder whether we should have Loopy share this evening for story time?"

Gran'ma answers quickly. "No, it will probably have to wait until tomorrow. I expect the meeting with Cydlo to be a lengthy one. In fact, I have already organized the evening meal and the kitchen crew. As usual, Stormy will take over ensuring things get done properly. And I suspect the meeting may then continue until way past story time."

Just now, some of the children are gathered around the dining table either playing board games or writing letters. The others are engaged in quiet conversation. Many of the children are quieter than usual. They have not yet fully recovered from the scary events of the morning when Gumpa opened his gift box.

Gumpa takes a final cup of tea as the tray is hurried away. He smiles to himself. *I'm proud of the children and their tenacious spirit to see things through to the end. They are not ready to give up yet.*

Barney arrives to announce that Cydlo is ready to start the meeting. He shrinks any of those who want to sit in and hear what's going on.

There are few signs in Twith Mansion of the chaos of the morning. Everything is back in its place, tidy and dusted. All the Little People, except Jordy, are present. He is covering the entrance in the absence of the toads.

Cydlo taps on the table top for the meeting to come to order. "Before we get into a discussion about the tunnel closure, I want to discuss the light in the ring. It was a close run thing this morning. Had it not been for the light in the ring, the battle for Gyminge might have been over before it ever started."

He reminds them of the remark Specs made earlier about the laser. "Activating the light seems to do with excitement. In this case, the trigger is my own excitement. But that isn't something that I can control. It's a response to things happening around me. I've been testing the ring outside in the open. The results have not been promising. So far, I have had no success in reactivating the laser. The laser will happen when my excitement rises to the proper level.

"When the light does focus into a laser, I must be ready to put it to work without a moment's delay. I'll point it towards the wizard's curtain and see what happens. With the closure of the tunnel, it begins to look as though our only hope for the Return to even get started is for the laser to slash the curtain into shreds and open up a way into Gyminge."

Gerald has doubts about that being the answer to the Return. "Sire, I am not sure we are meant to enter Gyminge through the curtain. In the Lore there is a reference to a land trail that passes through water. According to Dayko, that is the road into Gyminge. If my understanding is correct, the way back into Gyminge lies through the tunnel, not a hole in the curtain. We have no choice but to make a way through.

"There is more from the Lore to guide and encourage us. The child who will liberate and restore our kingdom will travel to Gyminge along that land trail. It will not be a Twith child that liberates the land but a Beyonder child. However, the Lore does not say whether it will be a boy or a girl. He or she will carry the Royal Flag of the Twith, which the children have already made for us. That child will be armed with the Royal Sword and the Royal Dirk. On the forearm will be strapped the Royal Shield. The child will be unconquerable, for the shield protects against all the magic of the enemy. The weapons are indestructible.

"I believe that you are right, Sire. The laser is, I'm sure, the key to the destruction of the curtain. That will happen when it happens, but we need to look again at the first line of the last verse of Dayko's Rime. I have been misunderstanding what Dayko's Rime is saying. We all have. It only became apparent what he really means when we heard from Loopy today that the wizard has built a wall at the Gyminge end of the tunnel.

"Do you remember when we went with Buffo to rescue gran'ma? We were sitting at the top of the waterfall climb, and while we were waiting for Buffo's return, we were looking down the tunnel to the small circle of light that marks the far opening of the tunnel. What does that tell us about the tunnel? It is simply that it is not crooked, it is straight throughout its length. What does Dayko's Rime say? Simply this.

The fall will lead straight to the wall.

"Can't you see? The wall in Dayko's Rime is not the wall of the castle as we have been thinking. It is the wall in the tunnel!

"That's right at the end of the poem! It's almost as though that is the final obstacle. It won't be what we shall encounter within Gyminge, but merely getting back into Gyminge at the border. Dayko saw all this happening, even what happened today. It will be a difficult path for us ahead, and victory isn't certain. But what we do know is that it has to be soon!"

The king nods his head. "Thank you, Gerald. That puts a different focus on things. We had several very eventful hours with the booby-trapped Jack-in-the-Box, the surprising light from the ring, the arrival of Loopy, and the news of the closure of the tunnel back into Gyminge. What do we make of it all?"

For a moment or two there is silence and then Austin speaks up. He is planning to be a mechanical engineer and his mind is quick and sharp. He shares his thoughts. "Well, we all know that what the wizard did by booby-trapping the Jack-in-the-Box was worse than anything that he has done before. But once again, he didn't win. He very well could have, but he didn't. I think there is something around us that protects us. There has to be! You think of all the adventures we have had since we first came to the farm. So many times things could have gone really, really wrong. But they haven't. We are getting closer now to the date for the Return. There is only one month left for everything to happen, but Dayko's Rime keeps on fulfilling itself. I'm sure we're on the right track. We just have to trust in the Rime and keep trying to understand it.

"I think Loopy is here for a very good reason. It is not just because of the dream that Pru and Nettie had about an explosion in the tunnel. It's because she was able to tell us about the wizard closing off the tunnel. We would never have known about that."

Micah throws in his idea. "What is in the pickle jar that the wizard placed in the tunnel? That's something we need to find out. I wonder if it is an atomic bomb. That would explain the dream. I don't much like the idea of being close to one when it goes off! But probably even a wizard couldn't fit one inside a pickle jar." He hesitates a moment. "Although I don't know about that. I suppose anything is possible with the wizard." He shrugs his shoulders and shudders.

Now Jenn speaks up. "The most important event of the day is the closure of the toad tunnel. It doesn't mean the Return is not possible. It merely means that we have to put together all the pieces of information we have and make sense of it. Somewhere amongst it all will be a clue to the next step. If we can't get into Gyminge any other way except through the tunnel, then we have to find a way to avoid the explosion and remove the wall the wizard built. We mustn't let time get away from us by not doing anything. We need to get moving."

Jock agrees, "Aye, we need ta move th' battle o'er inta Gyminge as quickly as possible. In th' meantime, we mus' remain continually alert."

Cydlo is thoughtful. "Yes, we do need to be vigilant for sure. As for the matter of moving the engagement with the wizard into Gyminge, that seems impossible at this point with the curtain closed and the tunnel now blocked."

Vyruss sits quietly, listening. He is remembering that Loopy said no lime or mortar is involved in building the wall. A daring idea forms in his mind.